# The Resurrection of Jesus Christ

Written & edited by

## Sean Ivory Garrett

(Through the inspiration of the almighty God and His only
begotten Son Jesus Christ, the Word of God)

# Dedications

To James Ivory Young & David Ivory Garrett

# Acknowledgements

To my wife Elizabeth,

Hector Catalan graphic designer & Leslie Sears

Cover design by Hector Mauricio Catalan

CatalanH@gmail.com

Edited by Leslie Sears

@Lesismore.us

ISBN-13: 978-0-9898817-0-8

Published by Sean Ivory Garrett

http://www.seanivorygarrett.net

Printed by

Createspace an Amazon Company

http://www.Createspace.com

# CHAPTER 1

## Jesus is accused by the Jews

For Pontius Pilate, the day started much like all other days. He spent much of his time in his office recording and documenting his notes, which were later sent to Rome as official periodic reports to Tiberius Caesar, supreme ruler of the Roman Empire. But the events which take place on this particular day, wouldn't only change Pilate's life forever, but would also revolutionize the modern religious world as it is known today. So how could Pilate predict the turn of events that would take place in his life on this day, and the days and hours following; the day Jesus was crucified, the man known as Christ?

Pilate held the position of Governor over the East Country, on the eastern most edge of the Roman Empire. He was esteemed prefect, first citizen of the Roman province at Jerusalem, in the common wealth of Judah.

Pilate sat at his desk in the early morning, deeply worried, addressing a letter to Tiberius Cesar, regarding the peculiar man whom was delivered prisoner to him over night. While up until now, he could not fully understand why Jesus had been brought to him in the first place. He reasoned that since Jesus was a Galilean, it was Herod's authority to oversee the prisoner and his subsequent trial that was soon to take place. But Herod returned Jesus to Pilate by the hand of Caiaphas and the Jews, and now it was Pilate's problem to deal with. Pilate, like all other people in the region, had heard of the greatness and the fame of Jesus, and all the miracles that accompanied him, and now he was responsible for the jurisdiction and litigation of his case and trial. All that Pilate knew, and had heard of the reputation and works of Jesus, made him a very strange man in Pilate's eyes. Pilate knew nothing of the Hebrew's religion; and their worship and practice was eccentric to him who knew only of the polytheistic gods of the Romans.

It started for him in the early hours of the morning, just prior to the first hour of the day (prior to 6 a.m.), before the sun's light had broken on the land, and darkness even now still ruled the sky. Pilate always used this early time before dawn to write his daily reports from the prior day.

He was addressing his first report to Tiberius Caesar, concerning Jesus whom he held prisoner, saying;

## To the most potent Tiberius, divine and awful Cesar, Pilate, Governor and administrator of the Eastern Province:

I have undertaken to communicate to thy goodness by this writing, though I have been possessed with great fear and trembling, most excellent king, the present state of affairs, as the events of yesterday have shown. For as much as I administer this province, my lord, according to the command of thy serenity, which is one of the eastern cities called Jerusalem. Wherein the temple of the Jews is erected, a great multitude of Jews, being assembled with the priests and elders, delivered up to me a certain man called Jesus. Bringing many and endless accusations against him; but have yet convicted him in anything. But they have one heresy against him in particular, that he said that the Sabbath is not their proper rest, [and has declared himself lord of the Sabbath]. Now this man has wrought many cures and good works. He also performed many cures on the Sabbath day of the Jews, and made the blind see, and the lame walk, cleansed lepers, healed the paralytic who were wholly unable to move their body or brace their nerves, but could only speak and discourse. He gave them power to walk and run, removing their infirmity by his word alone.

5

There is another very mighty deed which is strange even to the gods we have. He raised up a man who had been dead four days, summoning him again by his word alone, when the dead man had been decayed and his body corrupted by the worms which had been bred, and he had the stench of a dog. But, seeing him lying in the tomb he commanded him to run, nor did the dead man delay, but went forth from his tomb filled with abundant perfume. Moreover, even such as were strangers and demoniacs, having their dwellings in the deserts, devouring their flesh, and wandered about like cattle and all creeping things; he turned them into inhabitors of cities, and by a word rendered them rational, and prepared them to become wise and powerful. Being filled with every unclean spirit which was destructive to them, he cast them into the depth of the sea by the power of his word. And, again, there was another with a withered hand and half of his body was like stone; even him he healed with a word and rendered him whole. I have observed greater works of wonder done by him than by the gods whom we worship. But Annas, and Caiaphas, Gestas, Archelaus, and Phillip, with a multitude of priests and elders of the Jews have delivered him up to me, making a tumult against me that I might try him. Therefore being astounded by the terror of the Jews, being possessed with the most dreadful trembling, I have written what I have seen at this time and sent it to thy excellency;

## Pontius Pilate – Governor of Judah

He finished his report, and before the ink on the paper could dry, Pilate was tersely interrupted by a centurion, claiming that a multitude of Jews (Annas and Caiaphas being chief among them) had arrived again demanding an audience with him concerning the fate of Jesus. Only several hours before (it seemed) had Caiaphas and the Jews delivered Jesus to Pilate, now they were back wanting to proceed with the trial against him. He was disturbed not by the interruption of the centurion, but by the hasty manner of the interruption; he knew the issue of Jesus was present and their return was anticipated, but he did not expect the Jews to come back against him at least until tomorrow.

He ordered the centurion to see the Jews into the judgment hall. The centurion went out to greet the Jews as he was ordered. But when the centurion tried to lead Caiaphas and the Jews into the judgment hall, they stopped at the doorway of the entrance. They refused to enter into the Roman hall so that they would not defile themselves from eating the Passover, which was at hand.

Pilate took his time to organize himself. He finished writing, then signed and folded his correspondence to Tiberius and prepared it to be sent to him in Rome, then he went out into the judgment hall to hear the concerns of the Jews. Pilate was an experienced politician who had seen and been a part of numerous trials, but none of them were quite like the one he was going to experience this morning. As he walked out from his office to the judgment hall down the stone corridor, he felt apprehension and a moment of angst inside, but he did not fully regard the overture of the idea. He felt intuitively that this trial was going to be strange, even for the people of the Jews who he knew were well-prepared to accuse Jesus again with many heinous crimes.

As he entered into the judgment hall, he noticed their position outside of the hall (which appeared very unusual to him) as he walked up to his seat. Once he took his seat, he ordered the Jews to speak and state their claim against Jesus. Caiaphas, being chief among them, spoke for the multitude of Jews, and priests, and elders who came to accuse Jesus, saying, "We are assured, O Governor, that Jesus is the son of Joseph the carpenter, and born of Mary, but he declares himself to be the Son of God, and a king; and not only does he say thus, he also attempts the dissolution of the Hebrew Sabbath, and the laws of our fathers; Abraham, Isaac, and Jacob."

Pilate listened patiently to Caiaphas (which he was apt to do) then he replied plainly to Caiaphas' accusation against Jesus, "What is that which he declares? And, what is it which he attempts to dissolve?"

Caiaphas said to Pilate, "Our law forbids any to do cures on the Sabbath Day. But Jesus, the carpenter's son, cures both the lame and the deaf, and those afflicted with the palsy. He cures the blind and the lepers, and he even cures demoniacs on that day by his wicked methods."

Pilate said to him, "How can he do these things by wicked methods?"

Caiaphas answered, "He is a conjurer, and he casts out devils by the prince of devils, and so, all things have become subject to him."

Pilate said to Caiaphas, "Casting out devils does not seem to be the work of an unclean spirit, but to proceed from the power of God alone."

Then one of the Jews, Annas, who was the high priest of the temple that year, replied to Pilate saying, "We entreat your highness to summon Jesus to appear before your tribunal, so you can hear him for yourself."

Pilate paused for a moment, considering for a second Annas' proposition. Then he called out and signaled to his messenger who stood at the side of the judgment stand, and said to him, "By what means will you bring hither Jesus, whom is also known as Christ, I wish to speak with him as requests Annas the high priest of the Jews"? So the messenger went into the prison block. He had also heard of the great fame of Jesus. And he went in to retrieve him from his cell and bring him into the judgment hall, where Pilate was litigating the concerns of the Jews.

A multitude of Jews from throughout the countryside, knowing that Jesus had been arrested and delivered to the Governor, had now begun to come to the praetorium and quickly fill the small concrete judgment hall, inside and out. When the messenger opened the cell door to retrieve Jesus, he saw him sitting on the floor of the cell; and having heard of the fame of Jesus, and knowing the works that he committed among the people of Jerusalem, the messenger knelt down to his knees, at the foot of the cell, and worshipped Jesus, with submission and reverence. He took off the cloak that he wore around his shoulders, and spread the cloak upon the ground, and said solemnly to Jesus, "Lord, walk upon my cape and go in to see the Governor, for he calls unto you in the judgment hall."

So Jesus walked upon the cape, and walked down the hollow stone corridor, and he entered in the judgment hall where Pilate was deliberating with the Jews. And the messenger followed Jesus and also entered into the hall behind him, folding his cape, and shaking the dust of it off. But when the Jews saw the messenger folding his cape, they perceived his act of reverence toward Jesus, and Annas exclaimed against the messenger to Pilate, asking him, "Why did you not give Jesus his summons by a beadle, and not by a messenger? For the messenger, when he saw him, he spread the cloak that he had on his shoulders upon the ground and worshipped him, and said to him, "The Governor calls unto thee."

Then Pilate turned and called unto the messenger, saying, "Is what this Hebrew says against you true?"

The messenger answered, "Yes Governor."

And the Governor said to him, "Why have you done this act toward Jesus?"

The messenger replied to Pilate, "When you one day, my lord, sent me from Jerusalem to Alexandria, I saw Jesus sitting in a mean figure upon a she-ass, and the children of the Hebrews cried out to him, 'Hosannah', holding boughs of trees in their hands. And I saw many other of the Jews spread out their garments to him, saying, 'Save us, O Lord, thou who art in heaven. Blessed is he who cometh in the name of the Lord.'"

Then Caiaphas immediately interjected against the messenger, asking, "The children of the Hebrews made their acclimations to him in the Hebrew language no doubt. How could you, who art a Greek, understand the language of the Hebrews?"

The messenger answered Caiaphas, "I asked one of the Jews who I saw crying out, 'What is this that the children do cry out in the Hebrew language?' And he explained to me and said, 'They cry out, "Hosannah," which being interpreted means, O Lord, save me. Or, O Lord, save.'"

Caiaphas listened, but had no immediate response to the messenger's story, and Pilate quickly questioned Caiaphas about his silence, "Do you yourselves testify to the words spoken by my messenger toward Jesus,

Caiaphas, namely, because of your immediate silence?"
Pilate continued, "In what manner has my messenger done
amiss that he offends you so?"

Again, Caiaphas had no answer to Pilate and could
not refute the testimony of his messenger either. Not
convinced by the accusation of the Jews against the
messenger, Pilate ordered him to return Jesus to his cell. So
the messenger went forth and did as he was ordered, and
returned Jesus back to his cell. But as he led Jesus past the
ensigns, who carried the golden standards and the flag of
the Roman Legion, the heavy golden tops of the standards,
bowed themselves toward the ground in worship of Jesus as
he walked by out of the judgment hall returning to his cell.
And the Jews saw the ensign and the standard bearers
kneeling trying to maintain the weight of the standards as
they bowed themselves to the ground toward Jesus. And
Pilate saw the flags bow to the ground, as well, as did the
Jews and all those who were in attendance. And Caiaphas
and the other priests who stood in support of him,
exclaimed vehemently against the ensigns of the legion.

Pilate who saw the standards bow, responded to the
Jews over their fussing, "Is it not pleasing to you that the
standards did bow in worship of Jesus? Surely that is

something astounding to both you and I? But why do you exclaim yourselves against the ensigns who carry them?"

Caiaphas replied to Pilate, "We even saw the ensigns bowing and worshipping Jesus willingly."

The Governor turned and replied to the ensigns, "Why did you do this?"

And one of the ensigns who carried the colors of the Legion said to Pilate, "We only held the standards in our hands, as is our duty to do, and they bowed of themselves and worshipped as he walked past us. We could not resist the force of the weight of the gold of the standards." The ensign continued saying openly in front of the multitude of the people and Pilate, "We are all pagans, Governor, and we worship statues of stone as gods in our temples, how should we think anything about worshipping him who is alive and performs such miracles among so many people?"

Pilate then said to Caiaphas and the rest of the Jews, "If ye are not satisfied by the testimony of the standard bearers, do ye choose of yourselves strong men, from among your own people, and let them hold the standards, and we shall see whether they will then bend of themselves or not?"

So Caiaphas and Annas, and the elders of the Jews chose twelve of the most strong and able bodied men from among their people, and they made them to hold the standards of the Roman legion in the presence of the Governor. Then Pilate turned and called over to the ensigns of the legion and said to them, "I swear I will cut off your heads, if you have intentionally borne those standards in the manner in which you did when Jesus was led out of the judgment hall."

Pilate paused briefly, and took a short breath, trying to keep a clear perspective on the events of the trial so far, which had quickly escalated right before his eyes. He stood up and walked over to where the messenger stood and ordered him, "Take Jesus out of his cell again, and by some means bring him in into the judgment hall."

And the messenger left out of the hall to retrieve Jesus again, and when he opened his cell, he did to him as he had done the first time, insisting and entreating Jesus meekly that he would walk upon his cloak, for the Governor requests to see him. Jesus did as the messenger requested of him, and he walked upon the cloak and went in again to the judgment hall. And again, when he entered into the judgment hall, the Roman standards, carried this time by the strongest and most able-bodied men of the Jews, bowed themselves as they did the first time when the Roman ensigns carried them, and they bowed of themselves toward the ground and worshipped Jesus. Not even the strongest men of the Jews were able to resist the weight of the gold as they bowed of themselves.

At that moment Caiaphas and Annas, and the elders and priests of the Jews exclaimed more vehemently, this time against Jesus, claiming the standards bowed themselves by his wicked surmising. But all the people who had come and began to fill the small judgment hall, including Pilate, were amazed at what they saw, and they murmured in awe of the power of Jesus. Jesus, perceiving the hearts of the children, said to the Governor, "It is as David saith in the scriptures, 'God has spoken once; twice have I heard this; that all power is subject to the God of heaven.'"

# CHAPTER 2

Jesus is accused of being born through fornication

Now when Pilate saw the Roman standard's act of reverence toward Jesus, and when he heard Jesus speak for the first time, a look of concern came across his face. He was well aware of the reputation that preceded Jesus, and the concern flashed upon his face was tangible, it was perceived by his servants and soldiers that stood watch around the judgment seat where he presided; and noticed by those who stood aside and listened to the trial, but did not initially partake for fear of repercussion by the priests of the temple. By then, the judgment hall had started to fill with people curious about the fate of Jesus. Many of the people had followed him from Capernaum, and were rapt by the details of his impending trial.

Pilate started to rise from his judgment seat, but when he thought to get up, his wife Procla, who also stood at the side of the judgment seat, sent to him saying in an

17

earnest voice, "Have thou nothing to do with that just man, for he is innocent. I have suffered much concerning him in a vision this night."

When the Jews heard Procla testify this to Pilate, Caiaphas said to him, "Did we not tell you that he was a conjuror? Behold he has caused your own wife to dream of the evil of his surmising."

Pilate then turned to Jesus and asked him inquisitively, "Have you not heard the great accusations they say in testimony against you, and still you simply stand here and make no reply to them?"

Jesus said to Pilate, "If they did not have the power to speak, they could not have spoken. But because everyone has the command over his own tongue to speak both good and evil, let him look to it himself."

Annas answered out and said to Jesus, "What do you suppose that we shall look to, Jesus? In the first place, we know this concerning you; we know that you were born through fornication. We also know that upon the account of your birth, the infants, which were in Bethlehem were slain by Herod, all those male children under the age of two years old. We know that your father, Joseph, and your mother, Mary, had to flee into Egypt because they could not trust their own people to insure their safety from Herod the tetrarch."

Jesus looked and gave no answer to Annas, nor to any of the Jews' allegations. But several of the common people of the Jews had come down to the floor of the judgment hall and began to speak more favorably about Jesus to Pilate. One man interjected and said, "We cannot testify that he was born through fornication, because we know that his mother Mary was betrothed to our kinsman Joseph. And so, we say, that he could not have been born through fornication."

Pilate turned and said to Annas, "Your account that he was born through fornication, cannot be true, seeing there was a marriage and a supper, as this man testifies, who is of your own nation."

Caiaphas spoke insisting, "This whole multitude of people is to be regarded who cry out that he was born through fornication. They who deny him to be born through fornication are his proselytes and disciples."

Pilate asked Caiaphas, "Who are his proselytes?"

Caiaphas answered, "They are those who are the children of pagans, and are not become Jews, but are followers of him."

Just then, several other men among the common people stood forward and one of them replied angrily to Caiaphas and the priests, "We are not his proselytes, but children of the Jews who speak the truth, and we were present when his mother Mary was betrothed to Joseph."

Then Pilate addressed the common man who stood forward and testified, "I conjure you by the life of Caesar, that you faithfully declare whether he was born through fornication, and those things be true which you relate here now before me."

The man answered Pilate, "We have a law, whereby we are forbid to swear, be it a sin if we swear unto any. Let them swear by the life of Caesar that it is not as we have said, and we will be contented to be put to death."

Then Annas said, "These men will not believe that we know him to be basely born; and we know that he also pretends to be the son of God, and a king. We are so far from believing these things of him that we tremble when we hear them."

Having heard enough of the Jews' rhetoric for the moment, and trying to restore order to a divisive situation, Pilate commanded everyone in the judgment hall to leave out, except the men who testified that Jesus was not born through fornication. Pilate turned to Jesus and asked him to withdraw to a distance. But Jesus, already knowing his thoughts, turned and walked toward the back of the hall into the stone corridor. Pilate turned to the Hebrew men and asked them, "Why have the Jews a mind to kill Jesus?"

One of the men answered and said, "They are angry because he has wrought cures on the Sabbath day."

"Will they kill him for committing a good work?" Pilate asked.

# CHAPTER 3

## Pilate exonerates Jesus

Hearing the testimony of the common men of the Hebrews, Pilate was filled with anger against the Jews and went out of the judgment hall where they had congregated and said to them, "I call you to witness that I find no fault in that man."

Caiaphas replied to him, "If he had not been a wicked person, we would not have brought him before you."

"Won't you then take him and try him by your law?" asked Pilate.

Caiaphas answered, "It is unlawful for us to put anyone to death."

Pilate said to him, "Then the command therefore, Thou shall not kill, belongs to you and not to me."

Pilate then turned and walked back into the judgment hall where Jesus and the children of the Jews were waiting, and he called Jesus off by himself to ask him, "Are you the king of the Jews?"

Jesus answered him, "Do you speak this of yourself, or did the Jews tell it to you concerning me?"

Pilate answered with agitation, "Am I a Jew? The whole nation and priests, and rulers of the Jews have delivered you up to me. What have you done to them?"

Jesus said, "My kingdom is not of this world. If my kingdom were of this world, then would my servants fight, and I should not have been delivered to you by the Jews. But for now, my kingdom is not from hence."

Pilate said to Jesus, "Of what sort of a king are you?"

Jesus answered, "You say that I am a king. To this end was I born, and for this end came I into the world. And for this purpose I came, that I should bear witness to the truth. For everyone who is of the truth hears my voice."

Pilate said to him, "What is truth?"

Jesus said back to him, "Truth is from heaven."

"Therefore truth is not on Earth?" asked Pilate.

Jesus said to him, "Do you believe that truth is on Earth among those, who when they have the power of judgment are governed by truth, but form not righteous judgment?"

## CHAPTER 4

### Pilate finds no fault in Jesus

Pilate then turned to one of the centurions standing guard, and said unto him, "Show the priests of the Jews back up into the judgment hall." And, when the Jews had assembled outside of the doors of the judgment hall, Pilate said to them, "I find no fault in this man Jesus, that you have delivered up to me."

Caiaphas spoke again for the multitude of priests, "But, he said he would destroy the temple of God, and in three days build it up again."

Pilate asked, "What sort of temple is that of which he speaks?"

Annas said, "The temple at Jerusalem which Solomon was forty six years in building. He said he would destroy it and in three days raise it up again."

Pilate said to them, "I am innocent of the blood of this man, do you all look to it yourselves."

Then Caiaphas said to him, "Let his blood be upon us and our children."

Pilate said, "Do not act in this fashion toward this man, I have found nothing in your charges against him concerning his curing the sick persons or breaking the Sabbath, worthy of putting him to death."

Caiaphas replied again, "By the life of Caesar, if anyone be a blasphemer, he is worthy of death. But Jesus has blasphemed against the Lord."

Then the Governor turned again to Jesus and said to him in front of all the people, "What shall I do with you?"

Jesus said to him, "Do as it is written."

Pilate said back, "How is it written?"

Jesus said, "Moses and the prophets have prophesied concerning my suffering and resurrection. Even David the prophet said concerning me, 'But I am a worm, and no man; a reproach of men, and despised of the people.'"

The Jews hearing these words were provoked to an even greater anger, and Annas said to Pilate, "Why will you any longer listen to the blasphemy of this man?"

Pilate said, "If these words seem to you to be blasphemy, take him, and bring him to your judgment hall, and try him according to your law."

Annas shouted back, "Our law says, he shall be obligated to receive nine and thirty stripes, but after this if he shall blaspheme against the Lord again, he shall be stoned to death."

Pilate said to them again, "If that speech of his is blasphemy, then take him and try him according to your law."

But Annas said, "Our law commands us not to put anyone to death. We desire that he may be crucified, because he deserves the death of the cross."

Pilate replied to him, "It is not fit that he should be crucified; let him only be whipped and sent away."

Pilate looked out upon the common people that were present, and he saw many of them having great compassion toward Jesus. And he saw many of the women openly crying, and he said to the chief priests, "All the people here of your nation do not desire his death."

Caiaphas answered Pilate sternly, "We and all the people came here for this very purpose, that he should be put to death."

Pilate said to him, "But why should he die?"

Caiaphas said, "Because he declares himself to be the Son of God, and a King."

# CHAPTER 5

Nicodemus defends Jesus against the Jews

A certain man named Nicodemus, a Pharisee, and a ruler among the people of the Jews, a man of stature and austerity, stood before the Governor and spoke. He said to him, "I entreat you, o righteous Judge, that you'd show favor to me, and grant me the liberty of speaking a few words in your honor."

Pilate said, "Speak what you have a mind to speak, sir."

Nicodemus nodded his head in respect to Pilate, and said to him, "I, just yesterday, spoke to the elders of the Jews, and the scribes, and priests, and Levites, and the whole multitude of the Jews in their assembly concerning Jesus, and I asked them, 'What is it that you would do to this man? He is a man who has wrought many useful and glorious miracles in the midst of our people; in the land of our fathers, such as no man on earth has ever wrought before; nor will ever work. I advised them to let him go, and to do him no harm. I told them that if he comes from God, then all of his miracles, along with his miraculous cures will continue, but if they are only the works which come from him and not from God, then they will not continue. Just as our father Moses, when he was sent by God into Egypt, he wrought the miracles which God commanded him to do, even in the face of the presence of Pharaoh, King of Egypt, and all his magicians and counselors. Even though Janes and Jambres the magicians of Egypt, wrought the same type of miracles that Moses did by their own magic, yet could they not equally work all of the miracles that Moses did by the commandments of God. The miracles which the magicians worked, were not of God, as we know," directing his speech now at Caiaphas and the other priests. "But they who worked those works died, and perished, and all those who believed on them died with them as well. So now, I told them, let this man go, because the very miracles for which you have accused him of, are indeed themselves from God, and he is not worthy of death."

(This is the same Nicodemus who spoke to Jesus in private concerning the issue of being born again. He asked

Jesus, "How can a man be born again when he is old? Can he enter the second time into his mother's womb and be born?" And Jesus said to him, "Truly I tell you, except a man be born of water and spirit, he cannot enter into the kingdom of God. That which is born of flesh is flesh, and that which is born of spirit is spirit." This is the conversation that Nicodemus had with Jesus in private, not wanting to reveal himself as a disciple of his.)

But Caiaphas responded sharply to Nicodemus, "Are you now become his disciple by making speeches in his favor?"

Nicodemus responded sharply back to Caiaphas, "Has the Governor become his disciple as well? Does the Governor now make speeches for him also? Or, is Jesus innocent of the charges you brought against him? Did not Caesar place the Governor in this high position to be diligent and to make sound judgment? So why do you now question him and all the people who speak in favor of Jesus?"

Now when the Jews heard this speech coming from Nicodemus, they began to tremble and gnash their teeth at him, and their anger swelled inside them, Caiaphas and everyone that had come to see Jesus put to death. Annas came forth and said spitefully to Nicodemus, "May you then receive his doctrine for truth, and have your lot with your Christ" (being interpreted as messiah, or savior), stressing the name Christ with contempt, offended by the fact that Nicodemus stood to defend Jesus.

But when Annas spoke this, Nicodemus simply said to him, "Amen! I will receive his doctrine for truth and my lot with him, as you have justly spoken, Annas."

Just then, another Jew, an older man who himself was an elder, stood up and made his way forward, and quietly petitioned the Governor leave to let him speak a few words. And the Governor said to him, "Speak what you have a mind to speak, sir."

And the old man said to Pilate, "Righteous Governor; I myself lay for thirty-eight years by the sheep-pool, Bethesda, which is at Jerusalem, laboring under great infirmity, and waiting for a cure which should be brought by the coming of an angel, who at a certain time troubled the water. And whosoever first, stepped into the pool, after the troubling of the water by the angel, was then made whole of whatsoever disease he was afflicted with. But, when Jesus came beside the sheep-pool and saw me languishing there with no one to put me down into the water, he said to me, 'Wish thou be made whole by the troubling of the water?' And I answered him, 'Sir, I have no man, when the water is yet troubled, to put me down into the water.' And Jesus looked on me with great compassion, and said to me, 'Rise, take up your bed and walk.' And I was immediately made whole again by his words, and I took up my bed and walked as he commanded me to do."

But while the old man was speaking, Caiaphas interrupted and said to Pilate, "Lord Governor, I pray, ask this man what day it was on which he was cured of his infirmity."

The old man replied to Pilate, "It was on the Sabbath."

Caiaphas said, "Did we not say that Jesus wrought his cures on the Sabbath, and he cast out devils by the prince of devils?"

Then another man of the common people of the Jews came forth and said, "Lord Governor I have a mind to speak as well."

"Speak your mind," the Governor said to him.

And the man said in the assembly of all the people who had gathered themselves in the judgment hall, "I was once blind. I could hear sounds, but I could not see. And as Jesus was going along the road, I heard a multitude of people passing by, and I asked my neighbor who was passing? He told me that it was Jesus of Nazareth. And I cried out with a great voice saying, 'Jesus, Son of David, have mercy on me.' And Jesus hearing me stood still and commanded that I should be brought to him. I stood, and my neighbor lead me over to him, and he said to me, 'What is it that you will I do?' I said to him, 'Lord I will that I may receive my sight and see again as I did as a child.' And Jesus said to me, 'Receive your sight.' Presently, upon the moment he spoke his words, I regained my sight and I followed him, rejoicing and giving thanks to the Lord Most High."

Just then several others of the common people of the Jews began to come forth and testify to the miracles that Jesus had committed upon them, no longer afraid of what Caiaphas and the priest could conspire against them. One man claimed that he was once a leper, and Jesus healed him of his leprosy by his spoken word, just as he did for the others. Another man said that his body suffered from the palsy and that he stood crooked as a result, and

Jesus again cured him by his word alone, and his body was made straight. Also, a Hebrew woman, named Veronica, came forward and testified that she was afflicted with an issue of blood for twelve years, and when she saw Jesus she touched the hem of his garment, and immediately the issue of her blood stopped.

But Caiaphas and the priests and elders began to cry out against her, "We have a law that says a woman's testimony shall not be allowed as evidence."

But Pilate replied to them, "She is not being tried under your law, Caiaphas. Therefore, I will decide whether her testimony shall be allowed as evidence or not." Then Pilate turned to the woman and said to her, "Please, speak on." Then another man also came forward and claimed that he was at a wedding that Jesus was invited to (along with his disciples) in Cana of Galilee, in which Jesus commanded his servants to fill six pots with water and he turned the water into wine and all the people who were present at the wedding party drank with great astonishment at this miracle.

But another certain man of the Jews, a Pharisee, and a priest, who spent all of his time dedicated to worship and prayer, stood up and came forward and requested leave to speak on behalf of Jesus. And upon receiving leave of Pilate to speak in the assembly, he directed his speech to the Jews, saying, "I saw Jesus teaching in the synagogue at Capernaum; and there was in attendance a man who was possessed with a devil, and the man cried out to Jesus saying, 'Let me alone. What have we to do with you, O Jesus of Nazareth? Aren't you come to destroy us? For we know of a certainty that you are the Holy One come from God.' And Jesus rebuked the dumb spirit that possessed the man saying, 'Hold your peace unclean spirit, and come out of that man.' And at that present moment the unclean spirit came out of the man, and did no hurt to him. I've also seen a great company of people," continued the Pharisee, "come to see Jesus all the way from Galilee and Judah, and from the sea-coast, and also many countries beyond Jordan, and many infirmed people, and Jesus healed them all. And I myself have heard with my own ears, many unclean spirits crying out to Jesus saying, 'Thou art the Son of the living God.' And Jesus strictly charged them and commanded them that they should not make him known."

Then Pilate interrupted the Pharisee and asked him sharply, "And you swear by Caesar that your testimony and witness is true?"

The priest replied, "I swear to no power, other than the power of the almighty God. But if you find my testimony here today to be false, then let me be put to death this very hour."

Pilate, being filled with all fear and trembling stood and stared blankly, but intently, into the face of the Pharisee who spoke on behalf of Jesus, while many of the common people of the Jews, both men and women, stood and shouted in agreement, "He is truly the Son of God, who cures all diseases by his word alone, and to whom all devils are altogether subject to."

Pilate held up his hand to quiet the crowd of people who shouted out in the assembly, and he turned and said to Caiaphas and the multitude of priests and elders, "Why are not the devils subject to your doctors and priests?"

Caiaphas answered, "The power of subjecting devils can proceed from none but God."

Then Pilate said in return, "And doesn't that then prove him to be the Son of the living God, as you say (acting foreign and ignorant to the God to whom he refers) since the act of subjecting devils can proceed from none

37

other than the living God? Isn't he therefore the son of the living God whom the people declare him to be?"

While all the common people were aroused by the statements of the Pharisee, another man from among them, named Centurio, who had come from Capernaum, came forward during the trial and testified to Pilate that Jesus healed his son who lay at the point of certain death. And he testified to Pilate and all the people in and around the judgment hall intently listening to the trial, saying, "When I saw Jesus I said to him, 'Lord, my son lies at home sick with the palsy.' And Jesus stopped and said to me, 'I will then come to your house and heal him.' But I said to him, 'Lord, I am not worthy that you should come under my roof at this time, but only speak your word, and my son will be healed.' And Jesus looked into my eyes and said to me, 'Go thy way, son, and as you have believed, so let it be done to thee.' And from that hour my son was healed of the palsy and was again made whole."

Finally, exasperated from listening to the testimony of both the priests who accused Jesus, and the testimony of the common people who testified of his miracles, Pilate slowly turned toward the priests and elders, and said to them, "What will it profit you to shed the innocent blood of this man?"

# CHAPTER 6

Pilate sentences Jesus to be whipped & crucified

Then Pilate turned away from the Jews, and called together Nicodemus and the group of men who testified that they were present at the marriage of Joseph and Mary, the same men who testified that Jesus was not born through fornication. He said to them, "What shall I do, seeing there is likely to be an uproar among the multitude of the Jews and priests, who have come to see him put to death?"

One of the men responded to Pilate, "We know not what you should do concerning the fate of Jesus. We are not Governor, nor are we in a position to govern, let them (referring to the Caiaphas and the Jews) see to it who raise the tumult against Jesus. We have brought no charges against him."

Pilate then departed out of the judgment hall to where Caiaphas and the other priests had congregated, and he said to them, "You know that you have a custom, that I should release to you one prisoner at the feast of the Passover. I have a noted prisoner, named Barabbas, who has committed murder and shed much blood in the land; and I have Jesus who is called Christ, in whom I can find nothing in your charge against him that is worthy of death. Which one of them therefore do you have mind that I should release to you?"

Annas, Caiaphas, and the whole multitude of the Jews all cried out, "Release to us Barabbas!"

Pilate said back to them, "What then, pray you, shall I do with Jesus?"

The multitude vehemently cried out against Jesus saying, "Crucify him, crucify him," rousing themselves into a frenzy as they railed against Pilate to crucify Jesus.

Pilate was appalled by the fervent resistance of the Jews not to receive Jesus as their king. Jesus clearly was revered by the common people, who seemingly all were willing to testify to the miracles and goodness of his acts toward them and their kinsmen. Even Pilate himself was all but convinced of the innocence of Jesus against all the charges that the Jews had brought against him. Having spoken personally to Jesus, Pilate had not heard anything in his speech that sounded to him to be blasphemous. Many thoughts ran through Pilate's mind as he watched and listened to the Jews continue to rail against Jesus shouting, "Crucify him, He deserves the death of the cross."

It was for Pilate that rare moment when time slows down long enough for you to realize that you are experiencing something much greater than yourself. He looked into the faces of the Jews, the priests, and the elders and he had as much pity for them as he did anger toward their insolence. Just then, a lone anonymous voice cried out from among the crowd, which was simmering into an angry mob, "You are not a friend to Caesar if you release Jesus."

Then the people all agreed, and yelled more fervently against him in one accord. Another voice from among the mob agreed and shouted out, "Yeah, he has declared himself to be the Son of God, and a king. Are you inclined that he should be king rather than Caesar?"

Just then, the frustration that had been growing inside Pilate, finally exploded into an anger-filled tirade against what the Jews were attempting to do; Pilate began shouting at them, and saying, "Your nation has always been seditious, and you are always against those who have proven to be serviceable to you."

Then Annas shouted back to him, "Who has been serviceable to us that we have not listened to?"

Pilate replied angrily, "To your God, who delivered you from the hard bondage of the Egyptians, and brought you across the Red Sea as though it was dry land. He fed you in the wilderness forty years, with manna and the flesh of quails and brought water out of a rock, and he gave you a law from heaven to follow. To him you have been seditious. Instead of obedience, you provoked him with all your ways, murmuring against him and committing abominations in his sight. You even desired for yourselves a molten calf made of gold to worship instead of the living God. To the golden calf you made sacrifice, and you said within your hearts, 'These are our gods, O Israel, which brought us out of bondage from the land of Egypt.' On this account your God who created you for his own glory, was inclined to destroy you, as he did Dathan who rebelled against him most ardently in the wilderness, until even the ground opened up and swallowed him and all of his rebellious company. But the Lord's messenger Moses went before your God and made intercession unto him for your transgressions against him; and the Lord listened to Moses and forgave the iniquity of your forefathers. Yet and still, after all of that, all of you were again enraged against

43

Moses, as you are now against Jesus, and you would have killed him too, along with his brother Aaron. But they fled into the mountain to the tabernacle that the Lord had prepared for them. You have always murmured against the Lord's prophets, and you killed them as well who only sought to reckon to you the error and the destruction of your ways."

Stopping to collect himself from his tirade against the Jews, Pilate realized that he had over-stepped the bounds of his jurisdiction, and began to divulge knowledge of the history of the ancient people over whom he governed. It was something that happened very naturally as a result of his resentment, and also because he was very much a student of history and politics. But he paused and took a deep breath and walked back into the judgment hall.

He was inclined to banish the Jews completely from the praetorium, but as he started to walk back into the judgment hall, Caiaphas cried out, "We acknowledge Caesar to be king and not Jesus, for the reason that when he was born, wise men came from the east to offer gifts unto the child. But when Herod heard of this, he was exceedingly troubled in his mind, and sought to kill the infant Jesus. But Joseph, having heard of Herod's intent to

44

execute the child, fled with him and his wife Mary into Egypt. Then Herod, upon hearing the news that the child was born, instead of slaying the infant Jesus, he accordingly sent soldiers and slew all the children which were in Bethlehem, and all the sea coasts thereof, from two years old and under."

Now as Pilate listened to Caiaphas' speech, he became sorely afraid, and was overcome again with fear and anger toward the Jews. He then demanded that there be silence among the mob of Jews who were insisting that Jesus be killed, and he turned and walked over to Jesus who stood silently aside and said to him, "Are you therefore truly a king?"

Annas, hearing this, replied to Pilate, "He is the very person whom Herod sought to have slain."

But Jesus held his silence and did not respond to the allegations by the Jews that he should be put to death.

Then Pilate said again to Jesus, "Will you keep silence and not speak even to me?" Pilate paused to give Jesus a moment to respond, but Jesus held his silence even to Pilate. Pilate then replied with irritation toward Jesus,

"Do you not know that I have the power to crucify you, and the power to secure your release?"

Jesus looked at Pilate and responded to him, "You could have no power at all over me, except it be given to you from above. Therefore, those that have delivered me unto you have the greater sin."

Pilate listened and thought for a moment. Then he went out of the judgment hall and spoke again to the Jews, and this time, Pilate took water and washed his hands in front of all the people assembled in and around the judgment hall saying, "I am innocent of the blood of this just man. If you desire him to be killed, do you look to it among yourselves."

But Annas cried out, "If you let this man go, you are not a friend to Caesar. Whosoever makes himself a king speaks against Caesar."

Then Caiaphas spoke to Pilate the fateful words that sealed the fate of all those Jews, and priests and elders, who had assembled themselves together outside of the judgment hall against Jesus; he said, "May his blood be upon us and our children."

Pilate then said to Caiaphas and the other Jews, "Behold he is your king, should I therefore slay your king?"

But the Jews began to shout angrily, "Away with him, crucify him."

Pilate shouted again to them, "Shall I crucify your king?"

The priests of the Jews shouted back, "We have no king but Caesar."

When Pilate finished hearing the testimony of the Jews against Jesus, he was scared that he himself might become a victim of the angry mob of Jews who had assembled outside. He walked back into the hall and against his judgment and intuition commanded Jesus to be brought before his judgment seat. And Jesus walked to the front of the judgment seat where Pilate sat, and Pilate spoke to him, saying, "Your own nation has charged you as making yourself a king. Wherefore, I, Pilate, sentence you to be whipped according to the laws of the former Governors. Also, let it be that you shall be bound and then hanged upon a cross in the place of skulls, called Golgotha in the Hebrew tongue. You shall be whipped and crucified, you and the two criminals imprisoned with you, Dimas and Gestas."

Jesus said nothing and responded to Pilate with taciturn silence. Then Pilate ordered the centurions who stood guard over him to deliver him to the mob of Jews waiting outside in order to be whipped and crucified. So the centurions took Jesus and led him away to the mob of people waiting angrily outside of the praetorium. And as they led him outside many of the Roman soldiers who were present at the trial, began to mock Jesus, and several of them forcefully placed a crown of thorns upon his head, which tore right through his skin, and they mockingly put on him a purple robe, and said, "Behold the King of the Jews." Then, from that moment on, many people came and compassed and encircled Jesus as he stumbled through the streets of Jerusalem, mocking him, spitting on him, and beating him with their hands; some of them threw rocks and stones out of sheer resentment and hatred for him. Many in the crowd gaped upon him with their mouths as ravening and roaring lions, shouting curses and all manner of obscenities against him.

# CHAPTER 7

Jesus' crucifixion with the two thieves

Now as Jesus was led out of the judgment hall and whipped, then led up to Golgotha, the place of skulls, to be crucified and nailed to the cross, the mob that had compassed him stripped him of all his clothing and covered him with a linen cloth around his loins. Along with the crown of thorns that the soldiers placed on his head, they also put a reed in his hand as well, and they did likewise to the two thieves who were crucified along with him, Dimas on his right hand and Gestas on his left. And Jesus spoke to his God, saying, "My Father, forgive them for they know not what they do."

Now the four Roman centurions who gave watch over Jesus, took Jesus' garments and divided them into four parts, one for each of the soldiers, and his coat as well. But the purple coat that Jesus was wearing was without seam, and was woven from the top to the bottom and throughout the entire garment. So, the soldiers then reasoned among themselves, saying, "Let us not rend his coat and divide it amongst ourselves, but rather let's cast lots for it to see who shall possess it."

In committing this act, the soldiers fulfilled the scriptures as spoken of by David the prophet which said, "They parted my garments among them, and for my vesture they did cast lots." All these things the Roman soldiers did to Jesus just as it was written of them.

Just then, Pilate had come to Golgotha, leaving the security of his praetorium, and wrote upon a piece of wood the title, JESUS OF NAZARETH THE KING OF THE JEWS, in Hebrew, Latin, and Greek and secured it upon Jesus' cross. Many people of the Jews had read this sign which was written by Pilate because Golgotha was just on the outskirts of the city. But Caiaphas, the chief priest, who was among the mob of people who followed Jesus up to the top of the hill, said to Pilate, "Do not write, THE KING OF THE JEWS upon his cross, but rather write that he said, 'I AM the king of the Jews.'"

But Pilate answered Caiaphas saying, "What I have written, Caiaphas, I have written. And so let it be." And Pilate returned back to his praetorium in Jerusalem.

In the meantime, many of the people who stood by and watched Jesus, and had witnessed and heard the details of his trial, openly mocked him and said to him, "He saved others, let him now save himself if he can." Others said, "If he be the son of God, let him now come down from the cross and we will yet believe on him." Many of the chief priests, and elders, and Levites did likewise unto Jesus, openly mocking him and rebuking him.

The Roman soldiers also scorned Jesus, took gall and vinegar and offered it to him to drink, and said to him, "If you are the king of the Jews then deliver yourself." Even one of the thieves, Gestas, who was crucified along with Jesus, said to him, "If you are truly the Christ, then deliver yourself and us as well."

But Dimas, the thief who was crucified on the right hand of Jesus, rebuked Gestas, and said to him, "Do you not fear God, who is now condemned to this punishment? We indeed receive rightly and justly the demerit of our actions. But this Jesus, what evil has he done?"

After Dimas rebuked Gestas, with much pain and groaning, he turned and said to Jesus, "Lord, remember me when you come into your kingdom."

Jesus answered Dimas in a low agonizing voice, "Verily I say to you, that this day you shall be with me in Paradise, Dimas."

Now, there also stood by the cross, Jesus' mother, Mary, and her sister; along with Mary the wife of Cleophas, and Mary Magdelene. Also with them was one of Jesus' disciples, whom Jesus loved greatly. And when Jesus saw his disciple standing there, he said to his mother, "Woman, behold your son!"

And he looked at his disciple and said to him, "Behold your mother!" From that hour, the disciple took Mary, Jesus' mother, into his home, and treated her with the reverence and respect that a son does toward his own mother.

# CHAPTER 8

## The Miraculous Appearances at Jesus' Death

While Jesus and the two thieves lay agonizing on
the cross, the sun became eclipsed and darkness fell upon
the face of the entire earth. And even though it was noon-
time (the sixth hour of the day), people walked through the
streets of Jerusalem and all of Judah with lamps, as if it was
night. The stars that appeared in the sky, appeared, but their
natural brightness and radiance was not seen. And the
moon also appeared in the sky but its light was blocked out
and it looked as if it was tinged with blood. In that same
hour, the world of the dead and all those who were departed
from this world were swallowed up.

Now, while all of this was happening, the Jews who
remained inside the temple, and did not follow Jesus up to
Golgotha, saw that the sanctuary in the temple, where they
prayed and cast alms, did not appear to them; it vanished
and instead of the temple, a deep dark chasm in the earth

appeared where the sanctuary once stood. The priests who were in the sanctuary at that moment heard the sounds of successive rolling thunder coming from the darkness of the chasm. Great horror and terror overtook those priests who were in the sanctuary, as well as all the people who were throughout Jerusalem and all the countryside and were witness to the eclipse. Several of the priests who were in the sanctuary were swallowed up by the dark chasm that appeared in the earth where the sanctuary previously stood.

Many of the common people throughout the countryside saw the dead rising out of their graves and walking throughout Jerusalem as if they were alive. And the people who witnessed this murmured and said to one another, "It is Abraham, Isaac, and Jacob." Others said that they were Moses and the twelve patriarchs, and Job, who had died some three thousand five hundred years prior to this time.

Caiaphas, Annas and the other Jews of the temple who followed Jesus up to Golgotha were astounded and deeply troubled by the darkness and the sudden eclipse. They saw the stars appear in the sky without luster, and they saw the moon in the sky tinged with blood. And they realized at that moment that the scripture which spoke,

spoke of them. Then Caiaphas said fearfully to himself (and half to those priests who stood around him), "It is written, 'Let the sun not set on him that has been put to death.'"

Jesus, knowing that all things concerning him were now accomplished, and that the scriptures should be fulfilled, simply said, "I thirst."

One of the Jews standing there on Golgotha said, "Give him to drink the gall mixed with vinegar." Another Jew filled a sponge full of vinegar and gall and put it in his mouth. Upon doing this, the Jews fulfilled all things spoken of Jesus in the scriptures, and accomplished their sins against their own heads.

Those people who walked throughout the countryside with lamps fell down with their faces to the ground and wept for fear of the darkness and great evil that had come upon the land through the appearance of these miraculous signs. Many of the priests, who were at the sanctuary during the eclipse, were swallowed up by the opening of the chasm that they perceived in the earth. Most of those priests and elders, who opposed Jesus at the trial and condemned him to death, were consumed by great fear and darkness and many fell to their deaths into the pits of the chasm.

However, when Jesus received the vinegar he simply spoke and said, "It is finished." Then he cried out, "My Lord, My Lord, why have you forsaken me?" And when he spoke these words, he bowed his head and gave up the ghost. And immediately his spirit left his body and ascended up to heaven. It was about the ninth hour of the day when Jesus gave up the ghost, and the eclipse of the sun which started at the sixth hour, receded when Jesus gave up the ghost.

In that same hour, the veil of the temple that took Solomon forty-six years to build was split down the middle, tearing it from top to bottom. And the rocks in the earth were also ripped open. The graves of the dead opened up, and many more bodies of the saints, which did sleep, arose and appeared before many people who were in Jerusalem at that time. The eclipse of the sun that started in the sixth hour, shone no longer, and daylight was restored over the land.

Caiaphas and the other Jews on Golgotha, not wanting the bodies of Jesus, Dimas, and Gestas to remain on the cross because the Sabbath day was coming, sent message to Pilate and beseeched him to brake their legs so that their bodies could be taken away. One of the centurions who kept watch at Golgotha, broke the legs of both Dimas and Gestas. But when he came to Jesus to break his legs, he saw that Jesus was already dead and he did not break his legs. Another centurion who stood there grabbed a spear in his hand, and pierced Jesus' side, and immediately water and blood came pouring out from his body. Then the centurions who witnessed this, and bore record of these events, fell to the ground and began to glorify God. They said to themselves, "Of a truth, this was a just man, put to death without cause."

All the people who stood by and watched both near and afar-off, were exceedingly troubled at the sight of the miraculous events that took place while Jesus was being crucified. Pilate also witnessed the eclipse from his praetorium, and he saw the stars shine with no luster, and he saw for himself the moon tinged with blood. And they of the common people throughout Jerusalem, who witnessed first-hand the supernatural events at the time of Jesus' crucifixion, lamented with great fear and beat upon their chests, and returned back to their own homes full of fear and mourning.

Two of the centurions who kept guard over Jesus at Golgotha and witnessed the events of the eclipse, went to the Governor and related to him all that had come to pass, and all that they saw on Golgotha. Pilate made the centurions swear by the life of Caesar that what they testified was true. They both wrote and bore record of the events of the day as they witnessed them with their own eyes. And the witness of the centurions was documented and sent back to Rome as evidence of the miraculous events that took place at the time of the crucifixion.

When Pilate heard the testimony of the centurions, he became afraid for his own life because he realized that he wrongly put Jesus to death, who, for all intents and purpose, was indeed the king of the Jews. And Pilate reckoned within himself, that he could possibly be found guilty of killing and crucifying the son of the living God, which would surely be considered treason and would call for him to be beheaded. The possibility of treason was not an idea that he had ever imagined before in his life. Never could he see himself intentionally betraying his position as Governor and his allegiance to Cesar nor to the Roman Empire.

He contemplated seriously the fact that he helped to put to death the son of the living God, even though he knew Jesus was innocent of the charges that Caiaphas and the other Jews brought against him. It was this thought of the heavy burden of the responsibility for Jesus' death and what had taken place so far on this particular day that ultimately overcame him. Pilate fell to his knees, as did many others of the Jews who witnessed the same events, and he wept because through his actions that he committed, he realized that he helped to shed the innocent blood of Jesus, who many called Christ.

After moments of tears and anguish, Pilate gathered himself and began to replay the events of the trial in his mind over and over again, questioning what he could have done to save Jesus' life. He was convinced in his own mind that Jesus was innocent of the charges brought against him. He thought to himself that it would be best to call together Annas, Caiaphas and the Jews of the temple. And so he sent message that they should come immediately to meet with him in the praetorium.

Once the message was delivered, and they arrived at the praetorium, Pilate inquired of them about the events that had taken place earlier at the time of Jesus' crucifixion. He asked them, "Have you seen the miracle of the Sun's eclipse, and all the other things which came to pass, while Jesus was dying?" He asked them also, "Did you all see the stars shine without luster, and the moon which appeared in the sky tinged with blood?"

But as the Jews stood there and listened to Pilate, they were predetermined among themselves to conceal the facts of who Jesus was. Annas answered Pilate denying, "The eclipse of the Sun happened according to its usual custom."

Pilate was clearly perturbed by the Jews' denial of the eclipse. And he asked them again, "Did you not see the graves of the dead open up, and many of the souls of those who previously slept, walking throughout the streets of the city?" The Jews denied seeing the dead rise from their graves and walk about the city. So Pilate, already exhausted and bewildered by the events that had so rapidly deteriorated around him, knew already where the Jews stood on the issue of Jesus. He knew that they would deny anything which concerned Jesus (and him being the son of God), and he became irritated, and quickly sent them away.

He retired back to his office chambers where he started the day. He could not remove himself from the emotions of the trial, nor could he get the events of it out of his mind; neither the eclipse, nor the blatant denial of the Jews who continued to deny Jesus as their king even after all the miraculous events which took place, and were witnessed by all those who lived in and around Jerusalem and throughout the sea coasts.

Sitting in his office, taken with fear by the remarkable events, having to finally take in all that was happening, Pilate was again interrupted by a centurion who brought with him a certain man of the Jews. This time, it was not Annas or Caiaphas, nor any of the Jews of the temple, but a common man who introduced himself to Pilate as Joseph of Arimathea. Joseph was a disciple of Jesus', but not openly, for fear of retribution by the Jews of the temple. Joseph had come to Pilate in secret as well, to beseech the Governor to allow him to take the body of Jesus off the cross, and to give it a proper burial according to the Hebrew tradition. The Governor agreed with Joseph, and granted him permission to remove the body of Jesus from the cross, and to give it a fitting burial.

So Joseph left Pilate and went to the place of skulls to remove the body of Jesus from the cross, and with him came Nicodemus, who had defended Jesus on trial to Pilate against the Jews. Nicodemus was carrying a mixture of myrrh and aloes that weighed roughly one hundred pounds in weight. He intended in his heart to give the body of Jesus a proper burial, as did Joseph.

Many of the people who were acquaintances of Jesus stood at a distance, even the women who had followed him on the road from Capernaum. They had observed the hill from a distance, and all the events of the crucifixion, and all things that were done to Jesus by the people. They too witnessed the eclipse and all the miracles which had occurred that day. And, now, when they saw that Joseph and Nicodemus were intending to bury the body of Jesus, they reckoned amongst themselves that it was right for them, also, to bury his body. The people all agreed and gave their consent that the body of Jesus should be buried by Joseph and Nicodemus.

So the two men began the work of taking Jesus' body down off the cross, and the people watched and assisted. Joseph removed the nails from both his hands and his feet while Nicodemus and several others helped to secure his body. They felt first-hand the damage which had been done to his' body as it hung limply down over them; with all its bones being out of joint. They saw for themselves the large holes in his hands and feet from the nails which were hammered into to his limbs to fasten him to the cross. They saw the dirt from the sweat that accumulated on Jesus' face while he carried his cross up the hill to Golgotha, and the blood and bruises on his face and body which were suffered from the beatings of the people who were incensed against him. And they saw the deep cuts in his back and the skin around his skull from the whipping, and the crown of thorns that had been forcefully placed upon his head.

The two men took Jesus down from the cross with tears and anguish, and they planned to wrap him in linen cloths filled with myrrh, aloe, and all pleasant spices, according to the custom of the Hebrews. However, when they drew the nails out of his hands, and laid him upon the earth, the ground began to shake so that great fear fell upon all those who remained at Golgotha and throughout Jerusalem. The quake was felt throughout all of Judah and the sea coasts, even to Tyre and Zidon. It was felt even in the lands beyond Jordan and Egypt, and even as far away as Rome itself.

But the Jews who remained at Golgotha, the acquaintances of Jesus, who had followed him from Capernaum, and witnessed his crucifixion, rejoiced over his body. They gave thanks to their God for Joseph and

Nicodemus. They especially rejoiced over Joseph because they knew him, and they knew that he had witnessed many of the great things done by Jesus throughout all the cities of the Hebrews. Joseph and Nicodemus washed the body of Jesus, and rolled him in white linen cloth, and they brought him to his own tomb, in the garden which Joseph had purchased, and they laid his body in a tomb where no man had ever lay before. Then together they rolled a great stone into to the opening of the tomb, and they fastened it so no man could remove it.

The Jews, having returned back to the temple, saw the destruction of the temple that was caused when the foundation was rent from top to bottom while Jesus lay upon the cross and darkness came over all the land. They saw with their own eyes the actual destruction of the temple and how the earth moved and uprooted the foundation of it. The priests, and Levites, and elders, having witnessed Jesus' trial, and crucifixion, and all the miracles that happened while he lay on the cross, now saw the destroyed temple, and saw the sun returning to its natural order after the eclipse. They knew within their hearts that a great miracle had been set in motion through Jesus' death though they denied him to Pilate.

They listened to the reports from the other priests who remained in the temple during the crucifixion, and who saw the chasm that appeared in the earth where the sanctuary of the temple stood. They reported to Caiaphas and the other chief priests that many of their companions were swallowed up by the chasm in the sanctuary in the temple. But when Caiaphas and the others went in to see the chasm for themselves, they saw only the sanctuary as it was originally built by Solomon, and they did not perceive the chasm that had appeared and swallowed up those who were in the temple during the crucifixion.

Many of the priests who were in the temple and saw the chasm began to question what type of evil had come upon them and all of the people in and around Jerusalem. They had not yet realized that the eclipse of the sun (and the earthquake) was seen and felt throughout all the world, however. Having been intricately a part of the trial, and having witnessed the crucifixion; having been in and around the streets of Jerusalem, the priests heard the groans and murmurs of the people who walked about the city with lamps. They watched the people as they smote their breasts at the darkness of the eclipse and all the miracles, and openly fretted, "If by his death these most mighty signs have come to pass, it is apparent what righteous man he was."

The priests, and elders, and Levites again became afraid, but Caiaphas and several others hardened themselves against the miracles and they questioned what they should do to cover-up all that had transpired. They decided that they would send a message to Pilate, beseeching him to give them soldiers to guard Jesus' tomb for three days. The priests were men of great knowledge and dedicated their lives to the study of the scriptures. And they thought and realized among themselves that when Jesus spoke of rebuilding the temple, he spoke of the resurrection of the temple of his body, and not the temple made by mans' hands. So the priest set out from the temple and came again to Pilate, and they requested of him, saying, "Give us soldiers that we may guard his tomb, lest his disciples come and steal his body away, and all the people suppose that he is risen from the dead and seek to do us evil."

Pilate abdicated to their request and he sent soldiers to guard Jesus' tomb. He sent Petronius, a captain of the Roman Legion, and several soldiers under his command. The soldiers left to go set up their watch at the tomb, where

Jesus' body lay, having been cleansed and wrapped by Joseph and Nicodemus. Several of the priests of the temple went along with the soldiers to keep watch as well. When they arrived at the tomb, they set-up a small encampment outside of the sepulcher. Then they fastened the stones at the entrance of the tomb with seven seals, and pitched their tents and began to keep guard over the tomb.

Early on the next morning, while it was still dark, and the Sabbath day was drawing near, there came a multitude of Jews from Jerusalem and the regions round about it, intending that they might see the tomb where Jesus' body lay. As the night turned to day, many more people came to the tomb to see the place where Jesus' body lay.

All day long people came and went, to see the tomb where he was laid, praying and mourning over him well into the late hours of the night, on into the Sabbath day.

As nighttime fell on the Sabbath day, and the first day of the week drew near, the Roman centurions and several priests and Pharisees, continued to maintain guard of the tomb two by two, while the elders and priests and other soldiers slept. But, as the night hours moved on, and the darkness of the morning loomed, only two of the soldiers kept watch. And, at the sudden, the guards heard a resounding voice come from the eastern night sky, which had the sound of great thunder.

The centurions who kept guard turned and looked in the direction of the sky where they heard the thunder, and they saw the first light of the morning reveal itself in the sky. And upon this light, they saw the sky open up. The glow of the sun's light shone in great purple, and orange, and red lights, brilliantly illuminating the dark morning sky. When the centurions saw this light and the heavens open up, they immediately thereafter saw two men descending from the sky, glowing with a great white light slowly approaching the tomb where Jesus' body lay.

But those who were sleeping, were not awakened by the sound of the great thunder, and did not perceive the angels nor the brilliant light of the sun's glow.

The stone which was fastened in the entrance of the tomb rolled away of itself and made way in part for the two lighted figures to enter. And so they did enter into the tomb, and the centurions who witnessed it stood and stared in wonder and amazement, and they could not speak a word one to another. Dumbstruck, they slowly turned and thought to awaken the other centurions and the priests and elders, who were fast asleep; exhausted from keeping guard over the tomb for nearly three days with little sleep. As the other soldiers, priests, and elders began to wake from their sleep, the centurions who kept guard began to explain to them what things they had seen and heard in dark the morning sky. As the soldiers were explaining, there appeared three men who emerged from the tomb, and two of them were supporting the one by his shoulders, one on either side of him, and a cross was seen following behind the heads of them who emerged from the tomb. The light of the two heads of the men who supported the body, both reached up into the sky. But the light of the head of him who was led by the two men, was seen as over-passing the heavens.

Again a great voice was heard coming from heaven saying, "Has thou preached to them that sleep?"

And another voice was heard coming from the cross, saying, "Yes, Lord."

The centurions who stood guard, and initially witnessed the light descend upon the tomb, stood there astounded, as did the others, and not one person could speak a word, and great terror was seen in the eyes of the individuals who witnessed the lighted figures emerge from the tomb. But the centurions, ever mindful of their duty, considered one with another, whether to go and to report all they had seen to Pilate. While the centurions waited and thought thereon of what they should do, they saw again the heavens open up and a certain man clothed in white light descending from heaven and entering again into the open tomb, and he did not come out. And when the centurions and priests, and all those who stood around the tomb saw this, they hurried out of fear into the night to report to Pilate all they saw, as did the priests and elders who had been keeping watch. Many of the priests hurried away back to the temple to report to Caiaphas and Annas all they had seen while keeping watch at Jesus' tomb. Several others of the priests followed the centurions back to the praetorium.

When the centurions arrived at the Governor's compound, they found him in his living quarters, and they declared all the things that they seen that morning at the tomb. Pilate believed them because he also had heard the sound of the great thunder rolling in the darkness of the early morning sky. Being greatly distressed and overcome with fear, the centurions declared to Pilate, "Truly, Jesus was the son of God; and truly did we see men descending from heaven and enter into the tomb where he lay."

Then Pilate said to the centurions, "I am pure from the blood of the son of God."

But one of the Jews who followed the centurions to the praetorium said to Pilate, "But it was you who determined that these things should be done unto him."

While the centurions were reporting what they witnessed and discoursing with Pilate, the Jews who followed the centurions to the praetorium reasoned among themselves what they should do as well. They drew near to Pilate and entreated him, saying, "Lord, command your centurions and the soldiers who kept watch over the tomb to say nothing of that which they witnessed tonight. For it is better for us to be guilty of the greatest sin before God and not to fall into the hands of the common people who would surely stone us for what we have brought to pass against the land and all the people."

So Pilate reluctantly agreed to the terms of the Jews, thinking to himself that it would be all they deserved to fall into the hands of the people. But he said nothing, and he commanded the centurions and soldiers to also say nothing yet of the things they had seen that morning, and he sent them all away.

As dawn on the first day of the week turned to daylight, Mary Magdalene, a disciple of Jesus, appeared at the tomb with a small company of her companions who also believed on Jesus and wept for him as he was being tried, and whipped, and put to death. The women cautiously approached the tomb, and stopped to keep watch over it secretly from a distance, fearing that they would be caught by the priests and Pharisees whom they knew were burning with wrath against all those who supported Jesus.

The women came to the tomb intending to do the things which women are want to do for those individuals that die and are beloved by them. So Mary turned to her friends and said to them, "Since the day Jesus was crucified, we have not openly wept and lamented. Now let us do these things, and present our alms, and prayers for him."

One of the women asked Mary, "Who shall roll away the stone for us that has been placed at the opening of the tomb? For the stone is great and we being women cannot move it by ourselves."

Mary, being determined to give her due diligence to the body of Jesus, told her friends, "If we cannot lament and pray for him, we will set at the door the things which we brought as a memorial unto him. Then, we will openly weep and lament for him in the streets, and pray for him, until we have returned back to our homes." Mary's words satisfied the small company of women that came to the tomb with her.

When the women arrived at the tomb, they found the tomb opened and the great stone rolled away. When they came near to the opening of the tomb they looked in and there was a certain young man sitting in the midst of the tomb, who appeared to their eyes as a beautiful figure, more beautiful than anything they had ever seen before. He was clothed in a white robe of light, exceedingly bright. And the man spoke to the women, and asked them, "Why have you come here? Who is it that you seek?"

The women stood there confounded and unable to give an answer to the beautiful figure that sat before them. So he asked them again, "Do you seek him who was crucified? If you seek him who was crucified, he is not here. Of a truth, I tell you, He is risen again and has gone as it is written of him. If you do not believe my report, look in and see for yourselves the place where he lay, and you will see that he is not here." So the women looked into the tomb, and the figure said to them again, "He is risen and has gone where so ever he was sent."

Mary and all her companions, looking confused and dumbfounded, ran off from the tomb in disbelief to tell the apostles that someone had taken Jesus' body from the tomb. The women found the apostles all together, hiding themselves out of fear of being arrested by the Jews of the temple. And when the women arrived and found the apostles, Mary told them with great urgency, "They have taken the Lord out of his tomb and we know not where they have laid him." Immediately, Peter, Mary, and another disciple ran off to the tomb to see for themselves what had happened to the body of Jesus.

When they arrived at the tomb, they saw the man clothed in light sitting in the tomb, and the body of Jesus gone from where it was laid. The two apostles knew not, at that moment, what the scriptures said concerning Jesus, that he must rise again from the dead. And they looked into the tomb, and saw the linen that he was wrapped in together in a place off by itself. Then they saw the napkin that was placed on his head and loins, separated from the linen clothes, wrapped and folded together in a place by itself.

Peter and the other disciple, seeing that the body of Jesus was no longer in the place where it was laid, left the tomb and returned back to their homes dismayed and sorrowful, believing that the body of their Lord was taken from its tomb. But Mary waited at the tomb, and stood outside. And she fell to the ground at the entrance of the tomb, and she wept because she knew not what they had done with the body of her Lord.

As she looked again into the tomb, she saw two angels this time sitting inside. One of the angels was sitting at the head where Jesus laid, and the other sitting at the foot. One of the angels asked Mary, "Woman why are you crying?"

Mary responded, "Because they have taken away the body of my Lord, and I do not know where they have laid him."

But when she looked up again, Mary saw Jesus standing in front of her, but she did not recognize him, and she supposed Jesus to be the gardener. And Jesus asked her, "Why do you cry? Who is it that you seek?"

Mary said to him, "Sir, if you have labored to take and bury the body of my Lord, tell me where you have taken it, and I will own it from you and bury it myself."

Then Jesus said to her, "Mary."

And she looked a third time, and said to him, "Master."

She realized that the figure that stood before her was Jesus. When she realized it was him, she was compelled to embrace him, but he stopped her and said to her, "Touch me not, for I am not yet ascended to my Father. But go and tell my brothers, I ascend unto my Father, and their Father; and to my God and theirs."

Mary departed out of the tomb and ran back to tell the disciples that she had seen Jesus. She related to them the things he told her, and confirmed to them that Jesus was alive, and was going to ascend to his Father and theirs; and to his God," as he instructed her to do. The apostles, when they heard Mary's report, all cheered, and their spirits were renewed because of the good news that Jesus had been resurrected and Mary had spoken with him. And they were renewed by the fact that he had sent a message to them through Mary that he was going unto his father.

# CHAPTER 9

## Joseph gets arrested

The next morning, on the second day of the week, during the first hour of the day, before the sun first started to dawn, Pilate sat alone in his office chambers writing his daily report to Tiberius Caesar. Despite the extraordinary events that played out over the last couple of days, and despite his undeniable role in the death of Jesus of Nazareth, he was still a statesman, and he was expected to execute the duty and responsibility of his position as Governor. However, he was also a human being, a man, fallible in every way, and he was undeniably shaken by the supernatural occurrences surrounding Jesus' death, and the fact that he, to some measure of degree, was responsible for what transpired.

He found himself alone with his thoughts (trying to rationalize all that had come to pass, and deal with his own sense of culpability in all that happened), which continued

77

to be preoccupied by the miraculous events that had taken place over the weekend. He addressed his report to Tiberius, saying,

## Pontius Pilate to Tiberius Caesar the Emperor, Concerning Jesus who is called Christ – Greeting.

I have witnessed and received information most excellent one, in consequence which I am seized with fear and trembling. For in this province which I administer, one of whose cities is called Jerusalem, the whole multitude of Jews delivered unto me a certain man called Jesus, and brought many accusations against him, which they were unable to establish by consistent evidence. But they charged him with one heresy in particular, namely, that Jesus said the Sabbath was not a rest, nor to be observed by them. For he performed many cures on that day, and he made the blind to see, the lame to walk, and raised the dead, along with many other miraculous cures, curing each by his word alone. There is another very mighty deed which he performed which is strange to the gods we have; he raised up a man who had been dead four days, summoning him, again, by his word. Seeing the man lying in the tomb, he commanded him to run, and neither did the dead man delay, but he ran out of the tomb filled with abundant perfume. Again, there was another man who had a withered hand, and not only the hand but rather the half of the body of the man was like a stone, and he had neither the shape of a man nor the symmetry of body; even him he healed with his word and rendered him whole. And there was a woman also, who had an issue of blood for a long time, and whose veins and arteries were exhausted, and who did not bear a human body, but being like one dead, and daily speechless, so that all the physicians of the district were unable to cure her, for there remained not a hope of life within her. But as Jesus was passing by her along the road she mysteriously received strength by the passing of his shadow which fell upon her, and from behind she touched the hem of his garment, and immediately, in that same hour, strength filled her exhausted limbs, and as if she had never suffered anything, she began to run along towards Capernaum, her own city.

I have made known unto you these things which I have recently been informed of, and which Jesus did on the Sabbath. But Caiaphas, Annas, Archelaus, and Phillip, with all the people delivered him to me, making a great tumult against me that I might try him and put him to death. Therefore I commanded him to be scourged and crucified, though I found no cause in him for evil accusations or dealings. Now when he was crucified, there came darkness over all the land, and the sun was obscured for several hours during the daytime. And during the eclipse of the sun the stars appeared in the sky but no brightness was seen in them, and the moon also appeared and lost its brightness, and looked as if it was tinged with blood. Also, amidst the terror of the eclipse, the world of the departed was swallowed up and many whom did sleep, were raised from their graves. And I saw several of those who were raised from the dead. And many Jews who also saw them bore witness of them saying that it was Abraham, Isaac, and Jacob, and the twelve patriarchs, and Moses, and Job. And there were many whom I myself saw appearing in the body, who made lamentation over the Jews, because of the transgression which was committed by them, and because of the destruction of the Jews and their temple.

Now, after that, several Jews of the temple came to me and requested that I send soldiers to guard the sepulcher in which Jesus was buried. And on the first day of the week, while the soldiers were keeping guard, there came a sound from heaven, and the heaven became seven times more luminous than on all other days, and the sun lit up the entire hemisphere. Lightning flashes came forth in a storm, and there were men seen in the sky, great in stature, crying out, "Jesus who was crucified is risen again, come up from heaven ye that were enslaved in the subterraneous recesses of Hades." Their voices were heard as that of exceedingly loud thunder. And men were seen descending from heaven clothed with great white light and entering into the tomb. Even on that day, others saw the apparition of men rising again whom none of us had ever seen before. Therefore, being astounded by the great terror of the past three days, and being possessed with the most dreadful trembling, I have written what I saw at that time and sent it to thy excellency. The rest was reported to me by the centurions that I appointed to keep guard over his tomb, and I have inserted what was done against Jesus by the Jews, and sent it to thy divinity, my Lord.

## Pontius Pilate–Governor of the Eastern Province

Pilate sealed the letter and handed it to the centurion standing guard at the door of his office, so that the letter could be sent back to Tiberius Caesar in Rome. He sat down again at his desk and attempted to continue with his day just as before. But, Pilate knew within himself, that what he'd experienced and what he wrote in his correspondence had a profound affect on him; a lasting affect, one which any man would deem as life altering. He knew from the experience of the trial, and the subsequent crucifixion of Jesus that followed, he would not be the same person he was only days before. But how could he be the same? He had innocently put Jesus to death, the apparent son of God. And from the events that appeared in Jerusalem during the crucifixion, there was no denying the supernatural being of his righteousness, nor the fact that he truly was the son of the living God.

That same morning, Caiaphas and the unjust Jews returned to the temple and were congregating in the synagogue, debating the significance of the events that happened and what they should do from this point forward. Word had gotten back to them that Joseph of Arimathea had gone to Pilate in secret and begged him for the body of Jesus, and placed it in a tomb, in the garden he purchased with his own money.

Joseph's act of reverence toward Jesus enraged the Jews against him and they sent word to certain men that they were to find Joseph and bring him back to the temple. They also sought after Nicodemus who defended Jesus while he was on trial, and they sought the fifteen men who testified before the Governor that Jesus was not born through fornication, and all the other good persons among the common people who had shown and committed any good acts toward Jesus.

Word had already gotten back to Joseph that Caiaphas, Annas, and the priests of the temple were looking for him because he wrapped and placed Jesus' body in a tomb. The fifteen men and all the other people who defended Jesus at the trial all concealed themselves through fear of retribution by the priests and elders of the temple, and they were not to be found by the Jews. Only Nicodemus had the courage to show himself unto the Jews, and he went before them into the temple. And when he entered into the temple he again confronted Caiaphas and the rest of the priests, and again he spoke boldly and defiantly to them about Jesus, saying, "How can persons such as these enter into the synagogue of the temple after you unjustly put Jesus to death, knowing he was innocent of the charges you brought against him?"

But Annas answered Nicodemus and said, "How durst you enter into the synagogue who was once a confederate with Jesus? Let thy lot be along with him in the other world."

Nicodemus answered Annas, and said, "Amen; let it be so, that I may have my lot with him in his kingdom." Shortly after Nicodemus, Joseph had come to the temple, having heard that the Jews sought after him for burying the body of Jesus.

Joseph entered into the synagogue, and in like manner as Nicodemus, he confronted the Jews, and he spoke boldly to them as well, saying, "Why are ye angry with me for desiring the body of Jesus from Pilate? Behold, I, and Nicodemus with me, have put him in the tomb which

I have purchased, and wrapped him up in clean linen, and put a stone at the door of the sepulcher so that no man could enter. Surely, I have acted rightly towards him, but you all have acted unjustly against him who was just."

"In what manner did we act unjustly toward him?" asked Caiaphas.

Joseph responded, "In crucifying him, giving him vinegar to drink, crowning him with thorns, and tearing his body with whips; thus have you done and prayed down the guilt of his blood upon you and your generations,".

Upon hearing this, all the Jews who were in the temple at that moment became troubled and disquieted by the bold speech of Joseph. And they cursed him and gnashed their teeth at him. Then Caiaphas ordered the Jews who stood guard at the temple to seize Joseph. The guards apprehended him and took hold of him forcefully. Then Caiaphas commanded them to put him in the prison before the start of the next Sabbath day, and keep him there until it was passed.

While the men held Joseph with the intention to throw him into the prison, Caiaphas walked over to Joseph and confronted him. And he said to him, looking directly into Joseph's face, "Make confession, Joseph, for at this time it is not lawful to do you any harm until the first day of the week is come. And we know that you will not be found worthy of a burial. We will give your flesh over to the birds of the air and the beasts of the earth that they might consume you."

Joseph answered Caiaphas back and said, "That speech is like the proud speech of Goliath, who reproached the living God in speaking against David. But you priests and elders, and scribes and doctors, know that God said by the prophet, 'Vengeance is mine, and I will repay you evil equal to that which you have threatened unto me.' The Lord Jesus whom you have hanged upon the cross, is able to deliver me out of your designs, and all your wickedness will return upon your heads. Even the Governor, when he washed his hands said to you all, 'I am clear from the blood of this just person.' But you answered and cried out, 'May his blood be upon us and our children. According as you have spoken, may you perish forever.'"

The elders and the priests who listened intently to Joseph's words immediately became enraged against him. And they all began to scream, and push, and make tumult against Joseph, and several of the men who seized him, hit

85

him and began to beat him for speaking in that manner to the high priest Caiaphas and the elders of the temple. Then Caiaphas commanded the men to stop, and ordered those guards who seized him to remove him and take him down to the chamber and lock him up in the prison.

The men took Joseph down into the temple's prison and placed him in a cell that had only a tiny window sealed with bars in the top corner of the wall. Then the guards shut the iron bars that led into the cell and fastened the door, and sealed it with a lock. The high-priests followed the men down to the cell, seeing for themselves that Joseph was set in his cell, and they placed several guards just outside of the cell to keep watch, and they returned back to the synagogue. In the synagogue, the Jews took counsel for several hours with the other priests and elders, and they determined that they should all meet again after the Sabbath day, to determine to what death they should put Joseph. It was about the third hour of the day on the second day of the week.

Nighttime had fallen on the second day of the week, and the nighttime hours had pushed on into the early morning, and Joseph stood praying in the center of his cell and staring out of the barred window into the dark morning sky. The guards who were placed at the cell by the orders of Annas and Caiaphas all slept and were exhausted from keeping watch over the cell all night. While Joseph stood in the center of his cell praying, he saw four white lights descend from the sky and surround his cell, illuminating the place where he was imprisoned. He climbed up to the window to try to see where the lights had descended to, and when he stepped down, he looked back behind himself and he saw Jesus standing there in the form of a light as bright as the brightness of the sun.

He stepped down from the window and slowly fell upon the stony earth out fear of what was before him. But Jesus, laying hold on Joseph's hand, lifted him up from the ground, and sprinkled dew from the night air onto his face. Then Jesus wiped Joseph's face, and kissed him upon his head, and said to him, "Fear not, Joseph; look upon me for it is I."

Joseph looked up into the face of the lighted figure and said, "Rabboni Elias!"

But Jesus answered him, "I am not Elias, but Jesus of Nazareth, whose body you suffered to be wrappeded and placed in the tomb."

Joseph, not believing him to be Jesus, said, "If you are therefore Jesus, show me the tomb in which I laid you." So Jesus took Joseph by the hand and led him out through the bars of the cell where he was imprisoned, and the lock which was placed on the door remained untouched as if nothing happened and no one had come to open it. The guards who kept watch were wholly consumed by the spirit of deep sleep that had fallen upon all of them that same hour.

Jesus led Joseph to the place where he had laid him, and Jesus showed him the linen clothes, still wrapped and folded at one end of the bed where Jesus lay. And he also showed him the napkin that he wore on his head folded and separate from the linen clothes at the other end of the bed where he had once lay.

When Joseph saw the tomb empty, and the clothes wrapped separately from the napkin, he knew that the figure that led him out of his prison cell was indeed Jesus, and Joseph immediately worshipped him, and said, "Blessed be he who has come in the name of the Lord."

Jesus, again, taking Joseph by the hand, led him away to his own town of Arimathaea, and took him to his house, and Jesus said to him, "Peace be unto thee, Joseph;

but go not out of thy house until the fortieth day, for the Jews will surely be angered and astonished by your disappearance and send forth men to search for you. As for me, I must go to my disciples, and preach to them, and give them instruction to take out into the world, and tell the world of my crucifixion and resurrection."

So Jesus left Joseph and went to see his disciples, and Joseph rejoiced greatly and gave thanks to the God of heaven who had raised Jesus from the dead and had rescued him out of the hand of the Jews who were resigned to put him to death.

# CHAPTER 10

### The news of Joseph's escape

Early the next morning (3rd day of the week), Caiaphas and the other priests and elders assembled again in the synagogue after they had determined to what death they would put Joseph. Nicodemus came also to the temple that morning and assembled with Caiaphas and the other priests. Caiaphas ordered a messenger down to the prison block to retrieve Joseph from his cell. But as the messenger got down to the cellblock, he found the guard, who was appointed to keep watch over Joseph's cell, fast asleep, and he found Joseph mysteriously gone from his cell.

The messenger hastily woke-up the sleeping guard and asked him what had happened to Joseph and why he was not in his cell. The guard, who hadn't seen anything, and knew not that Joseph had escaped from his cell, was unable to give answer to the messenger, and told him that he hadn't seen or heard anything throughout the night. The guard told the messenger that he had fallen asleep in the last hours of the night, and that when he had fallen asleep, Joseph was sitting awake secured in his cell.

Neither of the men could account for what happened to Joseph; they both found the lock that was placed on the cell still sealed and secured on the cell door. It had not been removed nor opened as far as they could see. The guard still held on to the key that opened the lock on the cell door.

The messenger and the guard rushed back up to the synagogue to report to Caiaphas the news that Joseph had escaped from his cell. The messenger, when they got up stairs, reported to Caiaphas that the lock which was placed on the cell door had not been removed and was still locked and sealed upon the cell chamber, but Joseph had somehow escaped and was not in his cell. The messenger also told him that the guard keeping watch over the cell still held the key that opened the lock upon the door.

Now when Caiaphas and those assembled in the synagogue heard this news, they all went down to the prison block to see for themselves what had happened to Joseph, and found the same seal on the lock of the chamber. But, they could not find Joseph, and they all marveled and were astonished by the fact that Joseph was not in his cell but the lock was still securely fastened upon the door. So Caiaphas and Annas and the rest of the priests went forth again into the synagogue of the temple.

While they all wondered in amazement from the fact that Joseph had escaped, behold, one of the Roman soldiers who had kept watch at Jesus' tomb, came to them in the temple secretly and asked leave of them to speak in the assembly of the priests. Caiaphas granted him leave to speak and the soldier began to report to them all that he had witnessed while he was there, guarding Jesus' tomb. He spoke in the assembly and related to them his story from the morning on the first day of the week.

"While we were guarding the sepulcher of Jesus," he said, "we heard a great voice from heaven speak, and the voice that spoke had the sound of great thunder. And we saw two angels of God descend from heaven and roll away the stone which was placed at the entrance of the tomb, and when the stone was rolled away they entered into the tomb."

One of the elders present in the assembly asked the soldier, "What did these angels look like?"

And the soldier replied, "Their countenance was like lightning and their garments were as white as snow. And we saw the two enter into the tomb, and then shortly thereafter, we saw three figures emerge out from the tomb, the two supporting the one by their shoulders. And the head of him who was supported by their shoulders, compassed the heights of heaven. And we heard a great voice of thunder echo from the heavens."

Then as the soldier paused briefly Caiaphas interjected and asked impatiently, "What happened next?"

The soldier replied, "We who kept watch over the tomb became still and like those who could not speak, and through our fear we became like persons dead." Then we determined amongst ourselves that it was prudent that we should go to the Governor and report all we had seen to him. Several others among us went back to the praetorium, while I and one other stayed and kept watch at the tomb."

The soldier was noticeably shaken by the memory of what he was reporting to the Jews and one of the priests gave him water to drink and a chair to sit in. The Roman soldier sat and continued his story, "Later that morning we saw another angel descend from heaven and enter into the tomb, and we saw a group of women approach the tomb

93

where Jesus was buried. We heard the voice of the angel saying to the women, 'Do not fear, I know that you seek Jesus who was crucified; surely he is risen as he foretold you. Come in and see for yourselves the place where he was laid, and go presently and tell his disciples that he is risen from the dead, and that he will go before them into Galilee. There you shall see him as he told you.'"

Then Annas asked the soldier, "Who are those women to whom the angel spoke? And why did you not seize them as was your duty to guard the sepulcher?"

The soldier answered and said, "We knew not who the women were. Besides we became as dead persons through fear, and how could we seize those women?"

Annas replied to the soldier, "As the Lord lives, surely we do not believe you."

The soldier answered Annas and said, "When you saw and heard Jesus working so many miracles, neither did you believe on him, how should you now believe my report? And surely you have said well, for I am now convinced that truly the Lord does live."

Caiaphas sat there and thought for a moment, and then responded to the soldier saying, "You have said that you heard the angel tell the women that Jesus was going to go before his disciples into Galilee, is that true?"

"Yes, that is true," replied the soldier.

Caiaphas said to him, "Can you now therefore produce Jesus, whom you say has gone before his disciples?"

The soldier responded back to Caiaphas, "I have heard you say that you shut up Joseph who buried the body of Jesus in a chamber, under a lock which was sealed and when you went down to retrieve him he was gone. Is that true?"

Caiaphas said reluctantly, "Yes that is true."

"Do you then produce Joseph whom you put under guard in your chamber, and I will go and produce Jesus whom we guarded in the sepulcher," the soldier said.

Caiaphas responded, "We will produce Joseph, if you do produce Jesus." But, neither Caiaphas, Nicodemus, nor any of the other priests who were assembled that morning knew where Joseph was, and they knew not that he was now hiding in his own city of Arimathaea.

The priests and elders who were assembled in the synagogue were sorely afraid, and many did fear greatly as a result of Joseph's disappearance. They reasoned among themselves saying, "If by any means these things should become known amongst the people, then everyone would surely believe Jesus to be the messiah." They determined that it was better to pay the Roman soldier to keep secret all that had transpired that morning, and not to tell anyone of what truly happened.

So the Jews gathered together a large sum of money and told the soldier, "Go and tell the people that the disciples of Jesus came in the night while you were asleep and stole away the body, and if Pilate the Governor should hear of this story, we will satisfy him through our own means, and secure you." So the soldier took the money accordingly, and did exactly as he was instructed by the Jews; and his report was spread abroad amongst all the people.

Later that morning, three priests of the Jews, Phinees, Ada the school-master, and Ageus the Levite, came to Jerusalem from Galilee. They came to the temple to request leave to speak to Caiaphas and the chief priests and all who were assembled in the synagogue. Ada, the schoolmaster, addressed the assembled priests earnestly and said to them, "We have seen Jesus, whom you have crucified, this morning, talking with his eleven disciples, and sitting in the midst of them in the Mount of Olives. And we heard him saying to them, 'Go forth into the whole world and preach the gospel to all nations, baptizing them in the name of the Father, and the Son, and the Holy Ghost.' He told them that whosoever shall believe and be baptized, shall be saved. And when he had said these things to his disciples, we saw him ascending up to heaven in a light."

When the chief priests, and elders, and Levites heard these things they looked at each other in disbelief. They could not believe, and found it remarkable, that Jesus was rumored to be alive, as testified by these three men. Caiaphas said to them, "Give glory to the God of Israel, and make confession to him, whether those things which you testify be true, which you say you have seen and heard."

Phinees said to Caiaphas, "If we should not own the words which we heard Jesus speak, and that we saw him verily ascending into heaven, then we shall be found guilty, and our sin shall be upon us."

Caiaphas immediately rose up from where he was seated, and he gestured to several of the priests who were assembled there in the synagogue to bring out the book of the law, so that the three men could swear to the truth that they saw Jesus alive and heard him preaching to his disciples. And the priest retrieved the book of the law, and holding it in the hands of the three men, Caiaphas conjured each and every one of them saying, "You shall no more hereafter declare those things which you have spoken here in this assembly to anyone concerning Jesus."

The priests again gathered together a large sum of money, and gave it to the three men. And Caiaphas sent certain priests who should accompany the three men back to their own city, so that they might not by any means make their stay at Jerusalem and convince the people that Jesus had risen from his tomb and was seen preaching to his disciples in the Mount of Olives.

The priests, and elders, and Levites who remained in the temple, having expressed great fear and lament, questioned amongst themselves, "What extraordinary thing is this that has come to pass in Jerusalem as a result of the crucifixion and death of Jesus?"

But Annas defiantly attempted to persuade those priests against the testimony of the soldier and tried to comfort all those others who expressed doubt saying, "Why should we now believe the soldier who guarded the sepulcher of Jesus, in telling us that an angel rolled away the stone from the door of the tomb? Perhaps it is the case that Jesus' disciples told them this. Perhaps they too gave them money as well that they should speak such things, and they themselves took away the body of Jesus."

Annas continued presumingly, "Consider this brethren, there is no credit to be given to the foreigner, because he also took a large sum of money from us, and he has declared to all according to the instructions which we gave them. Either he must be faithful to us, or to the disciples of Jesus." But Annas was only speculating. He was not sure whether the soldier had taken money from Jesus' disciples or not, and neither could he wholly convince those priests who had begun to express doubt about the truth of the events that were unfolding around them.

# CHAPTER 11

## Nicodemus counsels the Jews

Then Nicodemus, who up to this point had kept quiet in the assembly and only listened with great intent, stood up and said to those priests and elders who expressed concern about the bizarre events that were occurring throughout the land. "You say right, O sons of Israel, because you have heard the testimony of those three men who have sworn by the Law of God, saying, 'We have seen Jesus speaking to his disciples upon the Mount of Olives, and we have seen him ascending up to heaven.' The scripture teaches us that the holy prophet Elijah was taken up to heaven, and Elisha, being asked by the sons of the prophets, 'Where is our father Elijah,' said to them, 'He is taken up to heaven.' And the sons of the prophets said to Elisha, 'Perhaps the spirit hath carried him away into one of the mountains of Israel.' And they reckoned that if they searched for him there perhaps they would find him. And the sons of the prophets besought Elisha, and he walked with them three days searching for Elijah and they could not find him. So now hear me, O sons of Israel, let us send men into the mountains of Israel, for perhaps the spirit has carried away Jesus, and perhaps maybe there we shall find him and our curiosity will be satisfied."

The counsel of Nicodemus pleased Caiaphas and many of the priests who had began to doubt what they had done to themselves by helping to convict Jesus and sentencing him to death. So they agreed to send forth men to seek after Jesus. And they sought after him in the mountains south beyond Bethlehem and Hebron, and others searched for him in the hills north on the other side of the Jordan River, but they could not find him. As the men sought after Jesus, certain of the priests found Joseph dwelling in Arimathaea. And when they returned to the temple, they informed Caiaphas that while they were looking for Jesus, they found Joseph instead.

The rulers, hearing this, as well as the people assembled in the temple, were glad and they praised the God of Israel, because Joseph was found, whom they shut up in a prison, and they still marveled and could not logically explain how he escaped. So the chief priests

101

called together all the priests, and elders, and scribes, and Levites and they gathered themselves together in a large assembly. They reasoned by what means they could bring Joseph back to the temple to question him to explain to them the miracle of his escape from prison. One of the priests who still doubted and feared, spoke up in the assembly again and said, "His escape came only by the hand of the living God and none other than that is apparent." So they decided to beseech Joseph to come to the temple by writing him a letter. Taking a piece of paper a scribe wrote to him and said,

**Peace be with you Joseph, and all your family**

We know that we have offended against God and thee. Be pleased to give a visit to us, your fathers, for we were perfectly surprised at your escape from prison, and great fear and doubt came over many of us who were assembled in the synagogue this morning when we discovered that you were gone. We know that it was malicious counsel which we took against thee, and the Lord himself delivered you from our designs. We pray that it will be expedient for you to come to the temple and explain to us the manner in which you were freed.

**Peace be unto you Joseph, who art honorable among all the people;**

And when they had completed the letter they chose seven men who were friends and companions of Joseph, and they instructed them that when they came to him, to salute him in peace and deliver to him this letter. When the men came to Joseph's house, they did accordingly as they were told and saluted him in peace, and delivered unto him the letter.

When Joseph read it, he said fervently, "Blessed be the Lord God, who has delivered me from the hands of the Israelites, that they could not innocently shed my blood. Blessed be our God who has protected me under his wings." And as Joseph rejoiced over his escape, he kissed the men who delivered to him the letter, and he took them into his house and prepared a feast for them to celebrate the Lord and his deliverance from the Jews. Joseph decided that on the morrow, he would prepare his ass and would return with them again to the temple at Jerusalem.

103

Now back at the praetorium, the soldiers and centurions confirmed to Pilate all they had seen on the morning of the first day of the week at Jesus' tomb. And they testified to seeing angels descending from heaven and entering into the tomb where Jesus did sleep. The soldiers also testified that they saw three figures emerge from the tomb, the two supporting the one by their shoulders. They told Pilate all about seeing the women who came to the tomb and what the angel told them about Jesus being resurrected and appearing unto his disciples in Galilee. For two whole days, since the first day of the week, many rumors had been reported to Pilate about the dead rising from their graves, many of whom he saw with his own eyes. And it was even reported to him that the disciples of Jesus had removed Jesus' body from the tomb.

But Pilate was still confounded by whether the stories he heard of Jesus being resurrected were themselves completely true. He knew that by whatever means, Jesus was like no other man that he had ever known or encountered before in his lifetime. And he knew for certain, by the witness of his own eyes, the great miracles that appeared in the sky over Jerusalem at the time of his crucifixion. But he was certainly not convinced of whether he was capable of believing that Jesus had come back to

104

life after being killed on the cross, and his lifeless body was wrapped and placed in a tomb. He suspected that it was possible that the rumors he heard about Jesus' disciples removing his body from the tomb, could perhaps be true. But as he sat in his office contemplating these ideas, several soldiers again came to him with more news that would force him to face his doubts and fears that the rumors of Jesus' resurrection were indeed true.

Several soldiers, who had been on their normal routine of duty throughout the countryside, reported back to Pilate that they of a certainty saw Jesus appearing in the body, walking and preaching to his disciples in Galilee. Pilate questioned the report of his soldiers, who all agreed in one accord that they had surely seen Jesus. And as the soldiers continued, they claimed that Jesus appeared in the same physical form in which they saw him at the trial, with the same disciples having not changed in appearance, and speaking with the same voice, and according to the same doctrine. The soldiers also claimed that when they heard him preaching he spoke this time with great boldness about his resurrection, and the coming of an everlasting kingdom.

Pilate's wife, Procla, again stood at a distance and heard the report of the soldiers that Jesus was risen from the grave and they had seen him in Galilee. She rejoiced over what she heard the soldiers report to Pilate because she believed in the visions which appeared unto her when the Jews delivered Jesus to Pilate to condemn him to death. But Pilate doubted nevertheless and was not wholly convinced in his mind by the report. He decided it would be best to send Procla up to Galilee to confirm the truth of Jesus' resurrection. So he sent with her Longinus (the centurion) and twelve soldiers, several of the same ones who kept watch at the sepulcher, and they went to greet Jesus face to face, as if they expected to see a great manifestation.

While they were riding from Jerusalem on the road to Galilee, the lead soldiers in the caravan saw again, of a certainty, Jesus walking along the road talking with several of his disciples. The company of soldiers stopped their horses at a short distance away as they saw him walking toward them, and they stared with amazement and great surprise that they were able to confirm with their own eyes that Jesus indeed was resurrected from the grave and alive again in the flesh.

As the caravan came to a stop, Procla saw Jesus. While Procla and the soldiers stood gazing and wondering at Jesus from a distance, he looked-up and he noticed the company standing there gazing at him in great awe. He saw Procla sitting inside the caravan, and he walked up to the company of soldiers and said to them, "Why do you look at me with such wonder?" Then he looked and noticed Procla, and he walked over to the coach where she sat. Jesus said to her, "Do you believe in me now, Procla, seeing that you behold me again in the flesh?" But Procla was unable to respond to Jesus when he spoke to her, and neither did the soldiers say but a word to Jesus.

Then Jesus directed his speech to her again and said, "Procla, know that in the covenant which God gave to the fathers, it is said that every body which has perished should live by means of my death, which you have witnessed just days ago. And now you see that I AM alive, who was once crucified."

Procla said to Jesus, "Is it truly you Lord, for I have suffered much in my dreams concerning your death?"

Jesus said back to her, "Surely it is I, Procla, and I have suffered many things also, even until I was laid in the sepulcher. But now hear me, and believe in my Father-God, who is in me. For through my death I have loosed the cords of death, and broke the gates of Sheol and the place of the dead. Thus my coming from henceforth shall be ever after."

Now when Procla, and the twelve soldiers, and Longinus, the centurion, saw Jesus in the flesh again for themselves, they could not deny the fact that he was present and standing before them resurrected from the dead. When they heard his voice and the nature of his speech, they began to weep with much sorrow. And the soldiers returned to Pilate weeping with heaviness and tears because several of them were the ones who were against Jesus, and devised many of the evils which were done against him the morning of his crucifixion.

Pilate, when he heard the news, fell upon his couch and he laid there in his bed of affliction. And he was scared. He lay there trembling, curled up like a child. He slowly turned to get up from his bed and put on a long dark garment of mourning. He walked over to his bed and he lay there scared, with the realization that all he had heard from Jesus while he held him prisoner and talked with him extensively, were indeed true. But the realization was the hard part, not just what he had heard from Jesus, but what was presently happening to him, and around him, due to the man Jesus.

Pilate slowly sat himself up at the edge of his bed, and he ordered the centurion who stood guard to gather to him fifty men, and prepare themselves to travel to Galilee so he could see for himself Jesus resurrected in the flesh. He slowly got up from the bed and began to put on his armor, when Procla noticed him readying to travel. When she saw the large contingent of soldiers assembling outside the praetorium, she asked Pilate where he was intending to go, and Pilate told her that he was determined to go to Galilee and see Jesus for himself. When Procla heard that, she was determined to travel along with Pilate to see Jesus again as well.

So Pilate and the soldiers set out for the city of Galilee. Pilate was anxious to confirm the truth of what he heard. He began to think about how this ordeal that he was now irreversibly a part of, should be Herod's responsibly since he was tetrarch of Galilee. He complained of this to the centurion who rode along side of him. Pilate cursed Herod to the centurion assuming that maybe Herod intentionally involved him in the legal matter to remove himself from all responsibility for what would happen to Jesus.

As they drew near to the city, the soldier leading the caravan of soldiers and horsemen saw Jesus at a distance standing along the roadside talking with his disciples. He held up his hand in order to signal the caravan of soldiers behind him to slow down. Pilate noticed the caravan slow its pace and he looked up to the lead captain and also noticed Jesus standing at the side of the road.

As the caravan of soldiers drew nearer to Jesus, they heard a great voice from heaven as the sound of dreadful thunder. And all of a sudden the earth began to tremble and shake all those who walked along the dirt road. Pilate's eyes became big, when he felt the ground shake. He looked at the captain who rode alongside him the caravan who too had a look and astonishment and fear. As soon as the quake stopped Pilate slowly began to step down from the caravan where he rode, and he walked out in front of his soldiers walking toward Jesus whom he saw talking to his disciples. As Pilate stopped and stood in the way of the road, Jesus turned and saw him then turned back briefly to continue speaking with his disciples. Pilate began to pray in his heart because he now realized that the man, Jesus, who was delivered to him that night, was the Lord of all created things.

As Pilate got close enough to see Jesus' face clearly, he bowed himself at Jesus' feet. Then Pilate thought and confirmed in his heart what was told to him by his soldiers; that Jesus had overcome the death of the cross, and had come back from the recesses of Hades. Now, when the soldiers and the captain of the soldiers noticed Pilate kneeling at Jesus' feet, the soldiers all stopped and slowly prostrated themselves with their faces toward the ground and bowed themselves also before the feet of Jesus.

Pilate slowly lifted his head before Jesus, and said to him, "I have sinned against you. I have sinned against him who avenges all in truth. And lo, I know of a certainty that you are God, the son of God, and while I held you prisoner I beheld your humanity and not your divinity. But I was constrained to do evil to you. Have pity therefore upon me, O God of Israel!" And when Pilate had said these things he fell back down with his face to the ground and wept openly before Jesus and his disciples.

Procla stepped down from the caravan when she heard the words of her husband, and walked toward Jesus and fell down to her knees at the feet of Jesus also, as did her husband, and said to him in great anguish, "O God of heaven and of earth, O God of Israel, reward us not according to the deeds of Pontius Pilate, nor according to the will of the children of Israel, nor to the thoughts of the sons of the priests, but remember my husband, Lord, in your glory."

When Jesus heard both Pilate and Procla, and he perceived the sorrow they felt because of what had been done to him, he commanded both of them to raise themselves up from the ground. And he commanded the soldiers to do likewise. Then Pilate, when he looked up at Jesus, saw on his hands and feet the scars that he suffered from the cross. And Jesus said to both Pilate and Procla, "That which all the righteous fathers hoped to receive, and did not see – in your time, the Lord of Time, The Son of Man, the Son of the Most High God, who is forever more, arose from the dead, and is now glorified on high, by all that is created. And, verily, as a truth, all is established forever and ever."

When Jesus finished saying these things to Pilate and Procla, he and his disciples turned and began to slowly walk again north up the road to Galilee. Pilate watched as Jesus and his disciples walked away in the night air. Procla then turned and embraced Pilate, he turned and wrapped his arms around her.

And they both walked back to the caravan where Pilate told the centurion to return them to Jerusalem. The soldiers took their charge from the centurion and turned their horses and the caravan around and slowly returned their Governor back to Jerusalem.

Early the next morning, Joseph woke up, him and the seven friends whom he took into his house, and he loaded up his ass for the trip back to Jerusalem. As the eight of them approached the city, one of the young priests who kept watch outside the temple saw them coming up the road toward the temple, and he ran into the synagogue to report to the high priests and elders that Joseph was with the men that they sent to retrieve him and bring him back to Jerusalem.

When the people heard these things they went out onto the road to meet him, and they cried out, saying, "Peace attend to your coming here, father Joseph." "Prosperity from the Lord attend to all the people," said Joseph. They kissed him and greeted him, and Nicodemus came also with them, and seeing Joseph he hugged and embraced him, and Nicodemus invited Joseph and all the priests back to his house where he would prepare a great meal and entertainment for them and all the people to attend knowing that Joseph was found.

So Joseph, and the priests and everyone at the temple that morning went to Nicodemus' house, and they all greatly rejoiced giving praises to the God of Israel for reuniting them with Joseph. As the people ate and exulted over Joseph's return, Annas began speaking with Joseph and said to him, "Joseph, please, make confession before the God of Israel, and answer to us all those questions which we are want to ask you about your escape from prison. For we were very much troubled, that you buried the body of Jesus, so much that we locked you in the chamber but later could not find you. Since the day of your escape, we have been afraid ever since, until this time of your appearance among us. Tell us therefore, father Joseph, before the Lord our God, all that came to pass and how you escaped from prison, for when we went to retrieve you from your cell, we saw the lock which we placed still fastened upon the door of the cell."

Joseph began to explain to the people who had gathered at Nicodemus' house, about his astonishing escape from prison, and he said to them, "You did indeed put me under confinement, on the second day of the week, until the next morning. But while I was standing at prayer in the middle of the cell, in the late hours of the night, the temple was surrounded by four angels and I looked with great wonder to see where they had gone. And so I looked but did see nothing. As I stepped down from my bed, I saw the Lord Jesus standing there in front of me as the brightness of the sun. When I saw him, I fell down to the ground with my face upon the earth for fear of him. But Jesus lay hold on my hand and lifted me up from the ground, and he sprinkled dew upon my face. He wiped my face, and kissed me and said to me, 'Fear not Joseph; look upon me, for it is I.' Then I looked up, and I said to him, 'Raboni Elias!' And he said to me, 'I am not Elias, but Jesus of Nazareth, whose body you did bury.' I said to him, 'If you are Jesus, then show me the tomb in which I laid you.' Then he took me by the hand, and led me out of the prison cell to the garden where I laid him in the tomb, and he showed me the linen clothes that I wrapped him in, and the napkin that I placed around his head.

"When he showed me the cloth that I wrapped him in, I knew that he was truly Jesus, and I worshipped him and said to him, 'Blessed be he who comes in the name of the Lord.' And again, he took me by the hand and led me to Arimathaea, to my own house. When he delivered me there

114

he said to me, 'Peace be unto you Joseph,' and he warned me not to go out of my house until the fortieth day, because he knew that you would be surely looking for me. Then he told me that he must go unto his disciples and give them the great commission to preach the truth unto the entire world, baptizing men in his name for the remission of their sins, because through his death he has taken away the power of death."

# CHAPTER 12

## Simeon's sons

When Caiaphas and all the chief priests heard the things that Joseph spoke of concerning his escape from prison, they marveled and all were astounded. Many, through the spirit of fear, fell to the ground and prostrated themselves to God, with their faces to the ground, and they said one to another, "What are these extraordinary signs that have come to pass in the land, by the death of Jesus? We know both his father Joseph and his mother Mary."

One Levite who was standing there dumbfounded by the fear of Joseph's story, said trembling, "I know many of the relations of Jesus. All of them are religious persons, who are often making prayers, and offering burnt sacrifices to the God of Israel in the temple." The Levite continued to tell those assembled at Nicodemus's house, "I was also in the temple that day when the high priest Simeon took Jesus as a baby in his arms and said to him, 'Lord, now let your servant depart in peace, according to your word. For my eyes have seen your salvation, which you have prepared in the face of all the people; a light to the gentiles, and the glory of your people Israel.' And when Simeon did this, in like manner did he bless Mary the mother of Jesus, and said to her, 'I declare to you, concerning this child, he is appointed for the fall and rising again of many, and for a sign which shall be spoken against. Yea, a sword shall pierce through his own soul, and the thoughts of many hearts shall be revealed.'"

The Jews who were listening, and heard the testimony of their fellow priests, knew that the things they spoke of were true, and that all these events which had taken place from the day of Jesus' crucifixion, were truly the works of God. But many of them remained hard-hearted against Jesus. Then Nicodemus stood-up and said to everyone, in a voice of calm and reasoning, "Brethren, let us send again to those three men, who said they saw Jesus talking with his disciples in the Mount of Olives." And Joseph agreed with Nicodemus.

Then Caiaphas confirmed the counsel of Nicodemus and sent out several men, to find those three men wheresoever they had gone, and bring them back to the temple to question them and confirm whether their stories of seeing Jesus preaching to his disciples were actually true.

Back at the temple, the priests retrieved the three men that testified that they saw Jesus speaking with his disciples in Galilee at the Mount of Olives and brought them again to Jerusalem. Upon their return, Caiaphas and the rest of the priests questioned them as to the exact details of what they saw concerning Jesus when he appeared before them in Galilee. The three men answered them all with one accord, saying, "In the presence of the God of Israel we confirm, that we all plainly saw Jesus talking with his disciples in the Mount of Olives, and ascending up to heaven in a light."

Annas and Caiaphas, still suspicious of the three of them, and their intentions, separated them, and had them all taken into separate rooms and examined individually. Each of the three men confessed the truth to the priests who questioned them and said that they had seen Jesus speaking with his disciples and ascending up to heaven. After each one of them was questioned individually and examined by the priests, the men were brought back into the synagogue, and Annas and Caiaphas were informed by the individual examiners of the responses of the three men. All of the priests who questioned them all related the same story as was told to them by the three men.

Caiaphas, realizing that what the men saw was the truth, said to the others, "Our law says, By the mouth of two or three witnesses every word shall be established."

But Annas responded to them indifferently concerning Jesus, still expressing disbelief of the testimony of the three men. Annas said to them, "But what is it that we have actually said about Jesus? We know that the blessed Enoch pleased God, and was translated by the word of God. And even the burying place of the blessed Moses is known. But this Jesus was delivered to Pilate, whipped, crowned with thorns, spit upon, pierced with a spear, crucified, died upon the cross, and was buried, and his body was buried by the honorable Joseph in a new sepulcher, and now these men testify that they have seen him alive. Moreover, these men have declared that they saw him actually talking in the flesh with his disciples in the Mount of Olives, and ascending up to heaven in a light, so they say. Maybe these three men are themselves the disciples of Jesus, and seek our destruction and the destruction of the Law of God."

Joseph stood up, and said to Annas, "You may indeed be justly under a great suspicion and surprised to hear, that you have been told that Jesus is alive, and he is gone up to heaven. For it is indeed a thing truly surprising to all who have seen and heard the stories that he is alive. But it is even a greater surprise to know that he should not only raise himself from the dead, but also raise others from their graves as well. Many of those whom he has raised have been seen by you and all the people in Jerusalem and throughout the countryside."

The priests who were in the synagogue at that moment, hearing Joseph's testimony, and the accounts of three men, all stood there in silence, including Annas, who was the most outspoken against them. But Joseph continued, "Hear me now, O priests and Levites, we all know the blessed Simeon the high-priest, who took Jesus in his arms in this very temple when he was an infant, and praised the God of our fathers. I tell you, that this same Simeon had two sons of his own, Charinus and Lenthius, and we know them, and we were all present at their death and funeral.

"I beseech you all here today, go therefore and see their tombs where they lay, for these tombs are now open, and these two men are risen from their graves. And, behold, they are presently alive and in the city of Arimathea spending their time in offices of devotion to the Most High God. I have seen them with my own eyes. Many indeed, have heard the sound of their voices in prayer, but they will not discourse with anyone. Rather, they continue in their devotion as mute as men dead."

Joseph then urged all those in the synagogue saying, "Come let us go to them, and let us behave ourselves toward them with all respect and caution and reverence to the Lord our God. Maybe it will be so that we can bring them here, and have them swear as an oath to us, and tell the truth about what they know. Perhaps, if we entreat them thus, they will tell us some of the mysteries of their resurrection." When Nicodemus and Caiaphas, and all the priests and Levites heard Joseph's speech, they themselves were emboldened and rejoiced exceedingly because they knew that Joseph was sincere and greatly esteemed amongst all the people.

So Nicodemus, Joseph, Caiaphas, and Annas, and several other priests set out for Arimathea searching for Charinus and Lenthius, the sons of Simeon. The first place they went was to their grave site, because they were all present at their death and funerals, but they did not find them there in their graves. Rather, when they arrived at the grave-site, they saw the graves of the two men both completely uprooted with a hole in the dirt where the bodies were laid.

So the group of men set out walking throughout Arimathea, and as they were going throughout the city, they found the two brothers, Charinus and Lenthius, on their bended knees worshipping and giving devotion unto God. The men all came near to them, and they saluted them, and they bowed themselves to the ground and worshipped the God of Israel as did Charinus and Lenthius. Each one of the men was humbled by the site of the two men resurrected in the flesh and worshipping God ceaselessly (even Annas and Caiaphas and the other unbelieving Jews). Joseph and Nicodemus saluted them with all respect and deference to God. And the others did likewise, and the men inquired of them to return back to the temple at Jerusalem so they could testify to them the mysteries of their death and their resurrection.

Charinus and Lenthius agreed and accompanied the priests back to the temple in Jerusalem. As they entered the temple they shut the gates thereof behind them, then they entered themselves into the synagogue, and Caiaphas sent men inside to bring out the book of the Law of the Lord. When they brought out the book of the law, the men put the book in both the hands of Charinus & Lenthius, and Caiaphas swore to them, saying, "By the God adonai, and the God of Israel, who spoke to our fathers Abraham, Isaac, and Jacob; by the law and the prophets, if you believe him who raised you up from the dead to be Jesus of Nazareth, tell us what you have seen, and how you were raised from the dead."

Charinus and Lenthius turned and looked at one another, and handed the book of the Law back to Caiaphas, and they began to tremble when they heard these things spoken to them by the high priest. The two of them were greatly disturbed by the request, and they groaned a deep groan of lament. Then they raised their heads up to heaven, and they both made the sign of the cross with their fingers on the tip of their tongues. Then, they looked back at Caiaphas and said to him, "Give each of us several sheets of paper, and we will write for you all those things which we have seen concerning our resurrection."

So Caiaphas summoned one of the priests to get pens and sufficient paper, and the two men sat down there in the synagogue, and they each began to write all the things they had seen concerning their death and their resurrection while they were held confined in the darkness of hell.

# CHAPTER 13

## The Narrative of Charinus & Lenthius

Before the two men began to record the testimony of what they saw concerning their death and resurrection, they spoke openly for all those assembled to hear, and they said, "O Lord Jesus and Father, who are God, also the resurrection and life of the dead, give us leave to declare your mysteries, which we saw after death, belonging to your cross; for we are sworn by your name; for you have forbid your servants to declare the secret things, which were done by your divine power in hell." After that, Charinus and Lenthius paused, and they were both led into separate chambers in the temple to record their testimony of what they witnessed in hell concerning Jesus and their resurrection.

When they sat down and started writing, they both started their testimony by saying, "When we were placed with our fathers in the depths of hell, amongst the blackness and darkness, all of a sudden, without warning, there appeared the color of the sun like unto gold, and a substantial purple colored light enlightened the entire darkness of hell. And it was so bright that we shielded our eyes from the glare of the brightness thereof. And immediately, upon seeing this, Adam, the father of all mankind, stood with all the patriarchs and prophets, and began to rejoice saying, 'That light is the light of the author of everlasting light, who has promised to translate all of us into his everlasting light at the coming of his word.' When Adam spoke those words, Isaiah the prophet cried out in a loud voice, 'This is the light of the Father, and the son of God, according to my prophecy when I was alive on earth. And I (Isaiah) said to the land of Zabulon and the land of Nephtalim, beyond the river Jordan, a people who walked in darkness saw a great light, and to them who dwelled in the region of the shadow of death, light is risen. Now he is come, and has enlightened us who sat in death, concluded Isaiah.'

"Now, while we were all rejoicing in the light which shown upon us (the two brothers wrote), our father, Simeon, came among us in hell, congratulating all the company, and saying to us, 'Glorify the Lord Jesus Christ the son of God. Whom, when he was an infant, I took him up into my arms in the temple, and being moved by the Holy Ghost I spoke to him, and I acknowledged him openly, and I said to him, "Now mine eyes have seen your salvation, which you have prepared before the face of all people, a light to enlighten the Gentiles and the glory of your people Israel."

All the saints who were in the depths of hell, hearing the voice of our father, Simeon, rejoiced even more. Then, thereafter, came forth another, one like a hermit, and he was asked by everyone, 'Who are you?'

To which he replied, 'I am the voice of one crying in the wilderness, John the Baptist, and the prophet of the Most High God, who went before his coming to prepare his way, to give the knowledge of salvation to his people for the forgiveness of their sins. And I John, when I saw Jesus coming toward me, being also moved by the Holy Ghost, I said, behold the Lamb of God, behold him who takes away the sins of the world. And I baptized him in the river Jordan, and I witnessed the Holy Ghost descending upon him in the form of a dove, pure and white. And I also heard a voice from heaven, saying, 'This is my beloved son, in whom I am well pleased.' And now, while I was going before him, I came down here to acquaint you all, that the son of God will next visit us, and as the day springs from on high, he will come to us, who are in darkness and, until this time, have walked under the shadow of death." In this manner John the Baptist concluded his testimony to the saints in hell.

## CHAPTER 14

Christ arrives at hell's gates

When Adam, the first man and father of us all,
heard what was told about Jesus being baptized in the river
Jordan, he called out to his son, Seth, and told him,
"Declare to your sons the patriarchs and prophets all the
things you heard from the archangel Michael when I sent
you to the doors of paradise to entreat God to anoint my
head with oil because I was sick."

And Seth came near to the patriarchs and prophets
in hell declaring to them, "I, Seth, while I was praying to
God at the gates of paradise, I beheld the angel of the Lord,
Michael, appearing to me saying, 'I am sent unto you from
the Lord. I am appointed to preside over all human bodies.
And I tell you, Seth, do not pray to God in tears when you
entreat him for the oil of the tree of mercy wherewith to
anoint your father Adam for his headache. Because you
cannot by any means obtain the gift of salvation until the
last days and times, namely, till five thousand five hundred

years be past. Then will Messiah, the most merciful son of God, come on earth to raise again the human body of Adam. At the same time, he will raise the bodies of the dead, and when he comes he will be baptized in the river Jordan. With the oil of his mercy he will anoint all those who believe on him. The oil of his mercy will continue to future generations, for those who shall be born of water and the holy spirit unto eternal life. At that time the Son of God, Christ Jesus, will come down on earth and will introduce our father Adam into Paradise, unto the tree of mercy. '"' This is what Michael the Archangel testified to Seth, the son of Adam at the gates of paradise.

When the patriarchs and prophets heard these things told by Seth, they began to rejoice with much cheering, exalting the Lord their God.

While all the saints rejoiced and praised the Lord for the everlasting light, which illuminated the dark halls of hell, satan, the prince and captain of death and Hades, spoke roughly to the prince of hell, commanding him, "Prepare to receive Jesus of Nazareth who is presently preparing to descend into our domain, and who boasted that he was the Son of God, and yet when he was alive, was a man afraid of death."

The prince of hell asked satan, "How do you know that he was truly afraid of death?"

Satan replied, "Because when Jesus was yet alive, he spoke, saying, 'My soul is sorrowful even unto death.' Also, he did many injuries to me and to many others of my companions. Even those people whom I made blind and lame, and all those whom I tormented with devils, Jesus cured by his word. Yeah, and even those whom I brought dead to you, he took them by force from you."

To this the prince of hell replied, "Who is that prince who is so powerful on the earth, and yet he is still a man who is afraid of death? All the potentates and kings of the earth are subject to my power!" exclaimed the prince of hell. "As are all those you have brought to me into subjection by your power, O satan. But I assuredly declare and affirm to you a truth, if Jesus of Nazareth be so powerful in his human nature such that, he is almighty in his divine spiritual nature, then no man can stand against him nor resist his power. Now, I assure you, when Jesus of Nazareth said unto you that he was afraid of death, his words were designed to ensnare and trap you, o satan. Unhappy will it be for you, and for your company for everlasting ages."

"Why do you now express such doubt?" replied satan. "And why are you now afraid to receive Jesus of Nazareth who is both your adversary and mine? I have done my work against him. What have you done to stand against him, o prince of hell? For I have tempted him and have stirred up my old people the Jews against him with anger and great zeal. I even sharpened the spear for his suffering; I mixed the gall with vinegar and commanded that he should drink it. I prepared the cross to crucify him, and the nails to pierce through his hands and feet. Now, his death is near at hand and I will bring him here to be subject to both you and me."

Then the prince of hell answered satan, "You said to me just now that he took away the dead by force? They, who have been kept here until they should live again upon earth, were taken away from here, not by their own power, but by prayers made to God, and their almighty God took them away from me. Who then is this Jesus of Nazareth that by his word alone has taken away the dead from me without prayer or supplication to God? Perhaps it is the same man who took Lazarus from me, even after he had been dead four days, and did both stink and was rotten, and of whom I had possession as lord of the dead, yet he brought him to life again by his power."

"Yes, indeed, it is the very same man", replied satan to the prince of hell. "Jesus of Nazareth is his name."

When the prince of hell heard satan, he said to him, "I adjure you by the powers which belong to both you and me, that you bring him not here to be subject to me. For when I heard of the power of his word, I trembled with fear, as did all my impious soldiers who were at the same time disturbed and dismayed with fear. Seeing that we were not able to detain Lazarus, for he but gave him a shake, and with all signs of malice and defiance, Lazarus immediately went away from us. Even the earth, in which his body was lodged, presently turned him out alive again. Now, as a result, I know verily that he is the almighty God who does perform such things. He is mighty in his dominion, and mighty in his human nature, and is the savior of all mankind who believe on him. Therefore bring not this person hither, for he will set at liberty all those whom I hold in prison because of their unbelief, and are bound by the fetters of their sins. All these he will lead into everlasting life.

While satan and the prince of hell were discussing the resurrection and divine nature of Jesus, and which one of them would receive him into their habitation, a voice was heard, as the voice of many thunders and great rushing wind. It was the voice of Jesus of Nazareth saying to satan and the prince of hell, "Lift up your gates, O ye princes of death, and be ye lifted up, O everlasting gates, and the King of Glory shall come in and visit you."

When the prince of hell heard the voice of thunder and of great rushing wind, he turned and said to satan, "Depart from me immediately, and be gone out of my habitations, o satan. If you are therefore such a powerful warrior as you say, who has dominion over the souls of the dead, then fight with Jesus, the King of Glory. But what have you to do with him, o satan? Be thou departed from me." And the prince of hell vehemently cast satan forth from his habitations deep in the dark recesses of hell.

Thereupon the prince of hell turned to all his impious officers who served him, and told them, "Shut the brass gates of cruelty and fasten them with iron bars, and now fight courageously against the King of Glory, lest we all be taken captive by his power."

When the company of saints who had been imprisoned in hell heard the command of the prince of hell unto his servants to fight against Jesus of Nazareth, they all began to upbraid him loudly with great anger, and speak boldly against his dominion, revolting against their captivity, saying, "Open your gates, o prince of hell that the King of Glory may come in." And David the prophet-king stood up and cried out against the prince of hell, "When I was alive on earth, did I not truly prophesize and say, "O that men would praise the Lord for his goodness, and for his wonderful works for the children of men. He has broken the gates of brass, and cut the bars of iron in sunder. He has taken them (the impious soldiers); because of their unrighteousness they are afflicted."

After this, the holy prophet Isaiah, spoke in the same bold manner as did the prophet-king David, to declare to all the saints, "Did not I rightly prophesy to you when I was alive on earth? The dead men shall live, and they shall rise again who are in their graves, and they shall rejoice who are in the earth. For the dew that is from the Lord brings deliverance unto them." I also spoke thus in another place, said Isaiah, "O death where is your victory? O death, where is your sting?"

When all the saints heard these things spoken by Isaiah and David, they railed even more vehemently against the prince of hell, saying, "Open your gates now, and remove the iron bars, for you will surely now be bound and stripped of all your power."

Then, again rose the voice of thunder and rushing winds coming from Jesus, and the voice said to the impious hosts of hell, "Lift up your gates now, O princes, and be ye lifted up ye gates, and the King of Glory, Jesus of Nazareth, shall enter therein."

When the prince of hell heard again the voice of thunder and wind, he perceived that indeed it was Jesus of Nazareth, and he cried out as though he were ignorant and knew not that it was the King of Glory, and he coyly answered, "Who is the King of Glory, that desires to enter herein?"

David the prophet, always valiant in battle, a man after the very heart of God, replied to the prince of hell, "Even I understand the words of that voice, because I spoke them by his spirit. Now, as I have said before, I say to you again, the Lord strong and powerful, The Lord mighty in battle, he is the King of Glory, and he is Lord in heaven and in earth." And the brazen speech by David, who rose up angrily in the spirit of the Lord, frightened the prince of hell and all his servants in their dominion; and David was emboldened and began to rail against all the hosts of hell,

"From heaven has he looked down to hear the groans of the prisoners in Hades, and to set loose those who are appointed to death. Now, open your gates thou filthy and stinking prince of hell, open your gates that the King of Glory may enter in; for he is Lord of heaven and of earth, and all powers have become subject unto him."

While David waged his war against the prince of hell, Jesus, the mighty, appeared in the form of a man, and enlightened all those obscure places in hell which had ever before sat in darkness. And he tore asunder the iron gates which were fastened at the entrance of hell, and the iron fetters which kept all the saints bound, which could not be broken even since now. He broke in pieces the chains and fetters that bound them to set free the captives in hell. Jesus, who was put to death and buried in the tomb, with his invincible power had now come and visited those who forever sat in the cavernous darkness of hell bound by their iniquity and the shadow of death by sin.

# CHAPTER 15

## Jesus confronts Death

The great voice of Jesus, the voice of rumbling and resounding wind, echoed throughout all the dark corners and caverns of hell. All those who heard its power were brought to fear at the coming of its destruction. And Death, who was mighty in his dominion, who no man had yet seen but all were subsequently captive to, and all his cruel officers, heard the power of the voice of thunder and were seized with fear in each of their several kingdoms once they beheld with their eyes the clarity of the light that entered into the domain. Death became blinded by the purity of the light, and Jesus himself suddenly appeared in the habitations.

When he beheld Jesus, Death therefore cried out with horror and said unto him, "We are bound by thee, O Jesus of Nazareth, Lord of heaven and hell, we know you intend our confusion before the Lord your God. Who are you? Who are you who has no sign of corruption, but rather has this bright appearance that is the full proof of your greatness, and yet you seem to take no notice of it? Who are you, so powerful yet so weak, so great but still so small in stature? Who are you, so mean and yet a soldier of the first rank who commands in the form of a servant, even as a common soldier? Are you that King of Glory, once slain upon the cross? Did you not lay dead in the grave, and are now come down alive for us to receive in our habitation?

"In your death all the living trembled, and all the stars were removed from their place, and now you have your liberty among the dead, and cause great disturbance among our legions. Who are you, O Jesus, who does release the captives that were held by original sin, and you restore them to their former liberty? Who are you who now spreads so glorious and holy a light over those who were made blind by the darkness of sin?"

In like manner, just as Death spoke to Jesus with trembling and fear, all the legions of devils in hell were seized with the same horror, and with the same passive fear they cried out to him, "When comest thou, O Jesus Christ, that now you are a man so powerful and glorious in majesty, so bright as to have no stain of sin, and so pure as to have no crime? For the lower world of earth, which was forever until now subject to Death and our dominion, and from them we received tribute, never has it sent to us such a dead man as you before. Never has the earth sent such presents as you to any of the princes of hell. Tell us now, Jesus, who therefore are you, who with such courage, enter among the abode of Death, and are not only not afraid to threaten us with the greatest punishments, but you also endeavor to rescue the captives from the chains in which we hold them? Who are you? Are you perhaps that Jesus Christ, of whom satan spoke to our prince, and by the death of the cross you were prepared to receive the power of death?"

But Jesus, standing in the midst of hell, in the brightness and fullness of his glory, could no longer bear the words of Death nor his angels, and he rebuked them all, and trampled upon Death with his feet, and choked him. Then he seized the prince of hell, and deprived him of all his power, condemning him under his dominion by the power of his words alone. Finally, Jesus sought out our earthly father Adam, and when he found him he embraced him and Jesus immediately ascended with Adam into the glory of his kingdom.

# CHAPTER 16

## Beelzebub & Satan

Then Beelzebub, the prince of hell, amidst all the confusion and destruction that ensued in hell at Jesus' coming, sought out satan. And when he found him, he grabbed him, and with great indignation he said to him, "O thou satan, prince of destruction, author of Beelzebub's defeat and banishment, the scorn of God's angels and loathed by all righteous persons, what inclined you to act this way against the King of Glory and bring him to our gates? Since you therefore intended in your mind to crucify him, through his destruction, you have made promises to us of great advantage which you could never deliver, and as a fool, you were ignorant of what determined destruction you have brought against yourself and all the dominions of hell. Behold now, Jesus of Nazareth, with the brightness of his glorious divinity, puts to flight all the horrid powers and armies of darkness and death. He has broken down our prisons from top to bottom, and dismissed all the captives. He has released all who were once forever bound, and loosed all who were want formerly to groan under the weight of their torments; but now they openly defy us and insult us. We are surely to be defeated by the prayers made unto their God. Our impious dominions are subdued, and no part of mankind is now left in our subjection.

"But on the other hand, they boldly disregard us to our faces. Never before now have the dead behaved themselves so insolently towards us; nor being prisoners, could they ever on any occasion be merry or cheerful in their spirits. Now they all openly shout their approval at the coming of Jesus of Nazareth. O satan, prince of all that is wicked, father of the impious, of the wretched and the abandoned, why would you attempt the exploit of Jesus of Nazareth, seeing that our prisoners were hereto always without the least hope of salvation and life? But now there is not one of them that does ever groan. Nay, on the contrary, they rejoice and exalt the Lord their God, nor is there the least appearance of tears in any of their faces.

"O satan, thou evil prince, keeper of the infernal regions, all the advantages which you did acquire by the forbidden tree, and at the loss of Paradise, you have now squandered by the wood of the cross. Your happiness and rulership on earth all but expired when you chose to crucify Jesus Christ the King of Glory. You have acted against your own interest and mine, as you will presently perceive by the large torments and infinite punishments which you are about to suffer. O satan, prince of all evil, author of death, and source of all pride, you should have first inquired into the evil crimes of Jesus of Nazareth, then you would have found out that he was guilty of no fault worthy of death. Why did you venture without either reason or justice to crucify him upon the cross, and bring down to our regions a person innocent and righteous, thereby losing dominion over all sinners, the impious, and all unrighteous persons in the under-world?"

While Beelzebub reprimanded satan for bringing Jesus down into the dominion of hell, Jesus again approached the two princes of the under-world, and said to Beelzebub, "Beelzebub, I have perceived the fear within your heart, and you have spoken wisely when you rebuked satan for his crimes against my person. Therefore, satan, the prince, shall be made subject to your dominion forever, in the room of Adam and the room of all his righteous sons who are mine."

# CHAPTER 17

Jesus ascends into Heaven with the Saints

Jesus left from Beelzebub and satan, and returned to find his saints and stretched forth his right hand to them and said, "Come to me all you my saints, who were created in my image, who were condemned by the tree of forbidden fruit, and by the devil and his lieutenant, Death. Live now by the wood of my cross. The devil, the prince of this world, is overcome, and Death is conquered."

Then quickly all the saints were joined together under the hand of the Most High God. And the Lord Jesus laid hold again on Adam's hand and said to him, "Peace be unto you Adam, father of all mankind, and to all your righteous posterity, who have come after you, which are mine."

Then Adam, being overcome with emotion cast himself down at the feet of Jesus, and addressed himself to

Jesus with tears, and with the most humble language, speaking in a loud voice he said to Jesus, "I will extol you, O Lord, for you have lifted me up, and have not made my foes to rejoice over me. O Lord my God, I cried unto you, and you have healed me. Lord, you have brought up my soul from the grave, you have kept me alive, so that I should not go down unto the pit." Then Adam stood up slowly and turned to all his sons and said unto them, "Sing unto the Lord, all ye saints of his, and give thanks at the remembrance of his holiness. For his anger endures but for a moment, and in his favor is life."

So, in like manner all the saints prostrated themselves at the feet of Jesus, and said with one voice, "You are come, O Redeemer of the world, and have actually accomplished all things through your death and resurrection, which you did foretell by the law and by your holy prophets. You have redeemed the living by your cross, and are now come down to us, that by the death on the cross, you might deliver us from hell, and by your power deliver us from death."

Adam then knelt on one knee in front of Jesus and again he was moved to speak before him and all the saints, and he said, "O Lord, as you have put the signs of your glory in heaven, and have set up the signs of your redemption even the cross on earth, so Lord, set the sign of the victory of your cross in hell, that Death may have dominion no longer."

Jesus did as he was requested of by Adam and he stretched forth his right hand, and made the sign of the cross upon our father Adam, and upon all his saints. And Jesus took hold of Adam by his right hand, and he ascended from hell up to his glory, and all the saints of God who were till then condemned to death and darkness followed him.

Whereupon the royal prophet David, while ascending up to heaven, boldly cried out in a loud voice, "O sing unto the Lord a new song, for he has done marvelous things (in heaven and in earth); his right hand and his holy arm have given him the victory over all those who made themselves his enemies. The Lord has made known his salvation unto his saints, his righteousness has he openly shown in the sight of the heathen."

After David the prophet-king spoke these things, the whole multitude of saints answered him and said at the top of their voices, "Praise ye the Lord! This honor has he bestowed upon all his saints, Amen!"

Then after the saints spoke in this manner, praising the God of heaven and hell, the prophet Habakkuk cried out with a joyful sound, "You went forth for the salvation of your people, even the salvation of your people, O Lord."

Then all the saints sang out again, "Blessed is he who cometh in the name of the Lord; for the Lord has enlightened us who has sat in darkness since the time of our death. This is our God forever and ever; He shall reign over us unto everlasting ages, Amen." In the same manner, all the saints and prophets continued to speak the sacred things of his praises as they followed Jesus into his glory.

# CHAPTER 18

## Jesus and the Saints in Paradise

Jesus, holding Adam by his hand, and leading his saints into the upper parts of heaven, delivered Adam to the archangel Michael. Then Michael led Adam and all the saints into the gates of Paradise, which was filled with the abundant mercy and glory of the Lord. When they arrived, two very ancient men met them there. When they beheld the two men, the saints asked them, "Who are you, who are men as we are, but have not yet been with us in the darkness of hell; but rather have had your bodies placed in the eternal light of paradise?"

One of the men, peering upon the saints, said to them, "I am Enoch, who was translated by the word of God, and this man who is with me, is Elijah the Tishbite, who was translated into paradise in a fiery chariot. Here we have hitherto been, and have not tasted the sting of death, but now stand ready to return to the earth at the coming of the Antichrist, being armed with divine signs, and miracles, to engage with him in battle, and to be slain by him at Jerusalem, and also to be taken up alive again into the clouds after three days and a half."

While the holy Enoch and Elijah were relating their mission to the saints, there came another man, in a miserable figure carrying the sign of the cross upon his shoulders. When the saints saw him, they questioned him inquisitively, asking, "Who are you? For your likeness is that of a thief. And why do you carry a cross upon your shoulders?"

To this question the man answered the saints, "You all say right, for I was a thief, who committed all sorts of wickedness upon the earth. And the Jews crucified me with Jesus, and I observed first-hand the unforeseen events that took place on the earth at the crucifixion of the Lord Jesus. I believed him to be the creator of all things, and the Almighty King. I prayed to him, and I said, 'Lord, remember me when you come into your kingdom.' And the Lord presently regarded my supplication, and he said to me, 'Verily, I say unto you, this day you shall be with me in Paradise.' And he gave me this sign of the cross, and he told me, 'Carry this sign and enter into Paradise, and if the angel who is the guard of Paradise will not admit thee, show him the sign of this cross, and say unto him the Lord Jesus Christ who is now crucified has sent me here to you.' I did this, and I told the angel who guarded Paradise all the things that Jesus told me, and when he heard them, the angels opened the gates and introduced me into Paradise, then he placed me on the right hand inside the gates of Paradise. Then the angel said to me, 'Stay here for a short time, until Adam the father of all mankind shall enter herein with all his sons, the holy and righteous servants of Jesus Christ, who was crucified.'"

When the saints heard this account from the thief, all the patriarchs said in one accord, "Blessed are you, O Almighty God, the Father of everlasting goodness, and Father of all mercies who has shown such favor to those who were sinners against him, and has brought them to the glory and mercy of Paradise, placed them in the midst of his large and spiritual provisions, in a spiritual and holy life; Amen."

# CHAPTER 19

## The Testimony of Simeon's sons

When Charinus and Lenthius finished writing the testimonies of what they witnessed in hell at the time of their resurrections, they folded and sealed their written statements and handed them to the priests who stood watch over the two of them while they separately recorded their accounts. Then both of the brothers were brought back into the synagogue before Annas and Caiaphas and the rest of the priests, and their testimonies were handed over to the high priests.

Charinus came forth and addressed all those who were gathered in the synagogue, including Joseph and Nicodemus, and he said to them, "These are the testimonies of the divine mysteries which we beheld and heard during our time captive in the darkness of hell. But, I, Charinus, and my brother Lenthius with me, are not allowed to declare the other mysteries of God which we saw, as was ordered to us by the archangel Michael. He reported to us, 'You shall go with the other brethren to Jerusalem, to serve as evidence of the resurrection of Jesus Christ, the King of Glory. And there, you shall continue all day in prayer and devotion unto God, declaring and glorifying the resurrection of Jesus Christ, seeing that he has raised you again from the dead on the first day of the week at the same time along with himself. And you shall not talk with any man, but rather sit as dumb persons until the time comes when the Lord will allow you to relate the mysteries of his divinity.' And the archangel Michael further commanded us to go beyond the river Jordan to an excellent and fat country, where there are others who also rose from the dead along with us for the proof of the resurrection of the body of Jesus. And now we have only these three days allowed to us to sojourn from the dead. We arose to celebrate the Passover of our Lord with our parents, and to bear our testimony for Jesus Christ the Lord, and we have been baptized in the holy river Jordan. Now all those who rose from the dead are no longer seen by anyone in the land, and only we remain among those who were once dead and now live by the stripes of the Lord Jesus."

"This is as much as God has allowed us to relate to you," said Charinus to those assembled, "Give you therefore praise and honor to the Most High God, O priests and Levites, and repent unto him and he will have mercy upon you."

So when they had made an end of their admonition to all the priests present in the synagogue, the guards who held onto their written testimonies, handed Charinus' copy to Annas, Caiaphas, and Gamaliel; and the other guard passed Lenthius' testimony to Nicodemus and Joseph. Then Charinus and Lenthius said with one voice, "Peace be to you from the Lord God Jesus Christ, the savior of us all. Amen, Amen, Amen." And when they prayed this upon all the people, immediately they were changed into exceeding white forms and were seen no more.

Upon seeing this all the people assembled at the synagogue stood astounded at the testimony and disappearance of the two sons of Simeon. Many of the priests who had once doubted, were now assured of their inclinations toward Jesus, and they were convicted in their hearts to the truth of his words which they heard for themselves, and the mercy of all his acts upon the people. All who stood around, including Joseph and Nicodemus were anxious and clambered to read the written statements that were handed in. So Gamaliel read first Charinus'

testimony to the assembly, and next Nicodemus read
Lenthius' written testimony. As they separately read them,
all the people gathered in the temple realized that the two
testimonies that were written agreed perfectly with one
another, word for word. Neither testimony contained one
letter more or one letter less than the other.

When the assembly of the Jews heard the surprising
revelations from the two brothers, some of them said to
each other, "Truly all these things were done by the
powerful hand of the almighty God, and he has blessed the
Lord Jesus forever and ever, Amen." Many of them at that
moment bowed their faces to the ground in subjection to
what they heard, knowing that Charinus and Lenthius
spoke not only of the world to come, but they lived and
experienced it as well, and now they were returned back to
where they had come from. Many of the priests fled out of
the temple with great concern, and fear, and trembling;
others smote upon their breasts, and went away, everyone
to his own home to mourn over Jesus.

Annas, Caiaphas, Gamaliel and a few other priests
stayed at the synagogue to see to the daily duties of the
temple. Joseph and Nicodemus slowly left out of the temple
just as the other priest did who all went away mourning and

lamenting. But as the two of them were leaving the temple, Nicodemus reasoned that it would be prudent for them to go to the praetorium to inform Pilate of all they'd seen and heard from Charinus and Lenthius this day. Joseph agreed with Nicodemus and the two of them went quickly to the praetorium to see Pilate.

When Jospeh and Nicodemus arrived at the praetorium, presently they were brought into the court-yard, outside of the judgment hall where the trial was held. They stood silently and looked at each other. The two of them briefly reflected on the events of the trial, while they waited for Pilate. When they were brought up to the Governor's office chambers, they immediately began to relate to him the accounts they'd heard from Charinus and Lenthius about the great dispute in hell between satan and the prince of hell. They also told him, with great clarity and detail, about the voice of thunder and rushing wind that overtook all the inhabitants and legions of hell with tremendous fear. They related to him the story of Jesus descending into the depths of hell with a brilliant light, and the color of the sun laden with gold and purple; and how Death and all the devils were in great horror at his coming. Joseph and Nicodemus tried to relate to Pilate as much of the testimony of Charinus and Lenthius as they could remember, because they both were still very much in awe of the depiction of the details they heard about life after death, and the works of Jesus in Hades.

Pilate was speechless but listened attentively to the story Joseph and Nicodemus were conveying to him. They discussed with him what they heard about Jesus destroying Death and putting him under his feet in subjection to his almighty power that he obtained through his resurrection, and how Jesus gave Beelzebub dominion over satan in his kingdom. Pilate was thoroughly astonished by what he was hearing from the two of them. In his mind, however, he almost didn't believe them; but he knew that all these things could possibly be accomplished by no other man than Jesus himself. He certainly knew not of any man in history, up until now, whom he had seen or knew of being resurrected back unto life. He had been through so much over the past week that he over-ruled his better judgment and let Nicodemus and Joseph finish their story of Jesus' descent into hell.

Pilate took it upon himself to record all the transactions and events reported to him by Joseph and Nicodemus, and he placed his notes in the hall of public records in the praetorium. Up until now, he had seen many strange things occur in Jerusalem where he governed the eccentric Jews, and he had seen and heard even more strange tales of the events that unfolded by means of the crucifixion of Jesus. But he had never heard stories about any man descending down into and returning from the depths of hell. He wasn't even sure what those concepts truly represented. He was no religious man, and had no knowledge of the Hebrew God any more than what he had heard and studied. He only venerated the gods of the Romans. But he knew that finally, the time had come, once and for all, for him to go confront Annas and Caiaphas. They were the high priests of the temple, and he would force them to reveal to him all that they knew about Jesus as testified to them from the holy scriptures. He knew that confronting them would certainly be contentious because of all the means the Jews had taken to deny Jesus to Pilate. They denied Jesus as being the king of the Jews, and they worked meticulously to discredit him and any of his followers.

Pilate called Longinus the centurion to his office chambers and told him to prepare his men to travel with him to the temple of the Jews. Longinus asked Pilate whether he should prepare a place for Procla, his wife, but Pilate denied his request. He wanted to confront the Jews, and he had no time to wait to summons Procla. His curiosity was now burning inside him. He had to confirm the truth about Jesus once and for all, to appease any doubt that was left in his mind about who Jesus truly was, and whether the Jews actually knew whether Jesus was the Christ and the King of the Jews.

# CHAPTER 20

## Pilate confronts the Jews

After taking in the account that was related to him by Joseph and Nicodemus about Charinus and Lenthius testimony of Jesus' death and resurrection from hell, Pilate gathered himself and got ready to confront the Jews at the temple and find out the truth of what they actually knew about Jesus, and what their books spoke of concerning his coming. While Pilate was thinking upon these things in his office chambers, Longinus the centurion entered again into his office, and told him that the soldiers were gathered and ready to depart to the temple. Pilate responded in kind to Longinus, and he and a small contingent of about twenty soldiers made their way through the streets of Jerusalem over to the temple of the Jews.

By this time, late in the afternoon, the sun was beginning to set on the day. After a short journey through the city, Pilate and the soldiers reached the gates of the temple and were met by the guards who kept watch over the gates at the entrance. Pilate, stepping out from the chariot where he rode, walked to the front of the caravan and spoke to the guards with all authority, "I am here to speak with Caiaphas and Annas," he said. "They are the high-priests this year, are they not?"

One of the guards who kept watch at the gate responded, "Yes, they are, Governor, how may I help you?"

Pilate responded, "My business is with the high priests, let me enter that I may speak with them about what they know concerning the fate of the man Jesus, who was crucified and risen from the grave on the first day of the week."

When Pilate spoke the name of Jesus to the guards, knowing full-well all the miracles that had taken place in and around Jerusalem at the time of his death, the guards, with visible fear on their faces, said to Pilate, "Enter, my Lord, and we will summon the high priests to whom you seek."

Pilate thanked the guards of the temple gates, and one of the guards sent another priest into the temple to retrieve Annas and Caiaphas. So the priest quickly hurried off into the temple and shortly came back with Gamaliel who immediately told Pilate to follow him into the temple. As they entered the temple doors, Annas and Caiaphas came forward and met Pilate, and Annas said to him, "We hear that you've come to speak with us concerning the fate of the man Jesus."

Pilate, eschewing any small talk, commanded the two of them, "Call together all the rulers and the scribes, and the doctors of the law that I may find out the truth concerning the death and resurrection of Jesus of Nazareth." So Caiaphas quickly departed and went and gathered all those priests, and scribes, Levites, and doctors of the law who remained in the temple that evening, and they led Pilate into a certain chapel of the temple. Pilate commanded them to shut all the gates of the temple, so that no business could be conducted and no interruption would come to the temple to lead the Jews away from the business that he had intended in his heart to do with them that evening.

So Caiaphas commanded the guards that the gates of the temple be shut. The gates of the temple were closed at Caiaphas' command, and the doors of the temple that led into the chapel were also closed, and only Pilate, Longinus, and several select soldiers stood inside the chapel walls where the Jews had taken them to hear what the scriptures said concerning Jesus.

Then Pilate spoke to the Jews and said, "I have heard that you have a certain large book in this temple, a collection of the writings of the priests and the prophets of your nation." Caiaphas responded to Pilate, in a voice intended to appease Pilate's apparent anger and determination to hear the words of the book, "Yes we have this book that you speak of, O Governor, what is it that we may do for you?"

Pilate replied, "I desire that this book be brought out and opened before me that I may know what it says concerning the coming of Jesus, the king of the Jews, who was crucified and risen from the dead on the first day of the week."

Caiaphas said, "It is not allowed for us to open this book except once a year, in which it is our custom to open in front of all the people that we may read of it and make

163

supplication to our Lord." Pilate at this point was well tired of the Jews subversion of the facts surrounding Jesus and was not willing any longer to bear their guile. Having put up with their craftiness for far too long, Pilate slammed his fist on the table which they had gathered around, and ordered Caiaphas again to have the book brought out and opened before him. Caiaphas, having no will to stand against Pilate concerning the matter of Jesus, turned and ordered several priests to go and bring the book of the priests and prophets that it may be opened to the conciliation of Pilate.

When the great book of the Jews was brought out, it was carried by four ministers of the temple. Pilate saw that it indeed was an especially large and heavy book, adorned with gold and precious stones, and he said to them all, "I adjure you by the God of your Fathers, Caiaphas, who made and commanded this temple to be built, where his name would stand throughout all ages, that you conceal not the truth from me any longer." At this, all those priests who stood there in the chapel looked at one another with astonishment and concern at how Pilate spoke to them with boldness and authority.

Then Pilate said to them, "You priests here know all the things which are written in this book, do you not?"

Caiaphas answered, "Yes we know a great many things which are written in this book, Governor."

Pilate then said to them, "Tell me therefore now, if you, in the scriptures have found anything concerning Jesus, who was crucified, and at what time of the world he was ought to come. If indeed you know these things, show them to me."

Caiaphas and Annas, having been sworn by Pilate to reveal all they knew about the time and the coming of Jesus, commanded all the rest of the priests who were with them to leave the chapel. Perceiving the weight and the gravity of the moment, the priests slowly filed out of the chapel and into the temple courtyard. Annas looked with apprehension at the contingent of soldiers who remained in the chapel, then he looked back at Pilate as to request the soldiers also to depart out of the chapel. Pilate turned to the soldiers who accompanied him and he commanded them to do the same and wait outside in the temple courtyard.

Only Pilate, Longinus the centurion, Annas and Caiaphas remained inside the walls of the chapel. As the soldiers left the chapel, Annas followed them and secured the doors of the chapel behind them. When he came back, Caiaphas said to Pilate, "You have made us to swear, Governor, by the building of this temple, to declare to you that which is true and right concerning Jesus. So let it be known that after we had crucified him, not knowing that he was the Son of the living God, we supposed that he wrought his miracles by some magical arts and not by the power of God. So we summoned a large assembly of priests, and Levites and doctors in this very room of the temple. And while we were deliberating among ourselves about the miracles which Jesus had wrought, we found many witnesses of our own country, who declared that they had seen him alive after his death, and that they heard him talking and discoursing with his disciples. They even testified that they saw him ascending unto the heights of heaven and entering therein."

Then Annas said to Pilate, "We even summoned two witnesses, men of our own nation, resurrected from the dead, whose father Simeon we did know, and whose funerals we were all present at. They told us many strange things that Jesus did among the dead; we have a sworn written account of their testimony in our possession."

Then Caiaphas said to Pilate, "Now, Governor, it is our custom annually to open this holy book before an assembly and to search out the counsel of God. And upon opening it and searching therein, we found in the first seventy books, where Michael the archangel was speaking to Seth, the third son of Adam the first man, an account that after five thousand five hundred years, Christ the most beloved son of God was to come to earth. He was to be proceeded by the prophet of the Lord," Caiaphas went on, "who shall prepare the way before him, and we perceived this prophet to be John the Baptist who did baptize the people in the holy river Jordan for the remission of their sins. We further considered, that perhaps, he who was to come, was the very God of Israel who spoke to our father Moses in the wilderness, saying, 'You shall make the ark of the testimony, two cubits and a half shall be the length thereof, and a cubit and a half the breadth thereof, and a cubit and a half the height thereof. By these five cubits and a half for the building of the ark of the Old Testament, we perceived and knew that in five thousand years and a half, Jesus of Nazareth, was to come in the ark or tabernacle of the body.' And so our scriptures testify that he is indeed the Son of God and the Lord and King of Israel," said Caiaphas.

167

"Therefore," he continued, "after his death and suffering upon the cross, and the many great signs that appeared in the heaven, more than a few priests of our nation were surprised because they knew that those events were wrought by means of his death. So we searched the scriptures and found the account of the creation, and at what time God formed the heaven and the earth, and the first man Adam, and that from then until the time of the flood were two thousand two hundred and twelve years. We reckoned also that from the time of the flood to Abraham was one thousand one hundred and twelve years. Then, we determined that from Abraham to Moses, were five hundred and thirty years. And from Moses to David the king were six hundred and ten years. And from David to the Babylonian captivity were another five hundred and fifty years. Finally, we determined that from the Babylonian captivity to the incarnation of Jesus were five hundred and fifty years. The sum of all these years amounts to five thousand and a half thousand years," said Caiaphas. "And as we reckoned from our searching the book of the Lord, and from the many signs that appeared in the heaven at the time of his death, that Jesus, whom we put on trial and petitioned for his crucifixion, is indeed Jesus Christ the

Son of the Living God, and he is true and Almighty; Amen."

This time Caiaphas and Annas were very direct and to the point in their revealing of the scriptures to Pilate, about what the prophets and priests had to say about the time Jesus was to come to earth. Pilate received the news from them in the same manner. He was very stoic in his expressions and mannerism. He allowed himself to stay quiet, and listen with great intent, while Annas and Caiaphas described in detail the words of the book to him. He certainly doubted in his mind whether Jesus was surely the son of the living God, which was the one issue that was the most heavily disputed by the Jews at his trial. And he knew, at the very least, that Jesus was the king of the Jews. Whether or not he was the son of the living God he was not completely sure of yet, but the facts were undeniable for him up to this point. He could no longer overrule the inclination of his reason. What he was hearing was profoundly devastating and enlightening at the same time.

Pilate held on to a bit of personal resentment toward Annas and Caiaphas and the rest of the Jews for threatening sedition against him at the trial. Their defiance at the trial was incessant, and he wondered at their ignorance and

169

persistence to crucify Jesus. But, he was nevertheless the civil administrator of this province, and his personal biases against the Jews had to stand at patience until he returned to his office and living quarters. But with his own eyes, just days earlier, Pilate saw Jesus resurrected and preaching to his disciples on the road to Galilee. He had spoken to Jesus and heard with his own ears Jesus' words at the time of his imprisonment and trial. Whether or not Jesus' words were blasphemy as the Jews purported against him, he did not particularly believe that to be true either. But now he was hearing the written testimony prophesied about Jesus of Nazareth from the book of the Lord, and there was no denying the truth of the words of that book. He knew full-well the strange stories of the miracles that had accompanied the Jews since they departed out of Egypt, and all the miraculous things that their God had done for them in their land. He witnessed the miracles in the sky at the time of the crucifixion.

It had all come to a head for Pilate. The truth about Jesus was now evident before him. Pilate took a moment and thought back to the words that Jesus spoke to him concerning truth, and he again realized within himself that this entire ordeal had now come full circle. His disbelief had given way to the reality that Jesus could be the son of the living God, which had given way to the fact that Jesus did indeed declare himself to be the King of the Jews, and all the things which were written of him in the book of the Lord.

With substantial heaviness, Pilate turned to Longinus, and signaled to him to retrieve the guards, and to ready his chariot and caravan to return back to the praetorium. He turned back to take a lasting look into the faces of the two priests, who stood together at the table behind the book of the Lord, and he marveled at the size and content of the book itself. He had no more use of questions or investigation to either Annas or Caiaphas. His experiences over the past several days, the personal time he spent discoursing with Jesus, the witness of Joseph and Nicodemus, along with the testimony of the book of the Lord, certainly dissuaded Pilate of all his uncertainties, and answered all unanswered questions that had lingered inside him since the day of the trial.

He stared blankly at Annas and Caiaphas. Caiaphas asked him before he could speak, "Does our declaration satisfy your inquisition lord Governor?"

Pilate responded to Caiaphas, "Yes, indeed it does. May your God see to the justification of your works against

Jesus, your king, as you have testified in his behalf from the book of your prophets." And with that he slowly turned and walked toward the wood and iron clad door where the Centurion Longinus now stood waiting for him. Before he exited he turned again to look briefly back at Annas and Caiaphas standing in the chapel with the book of the Lord opened before them, and he walked out into the court yard past the priests who stood patiently outside. He gave the command to his soldiers and loaded himself into his chariot. The small contingent of soldiers followed behind him in their caravan of horses and they returned Pilate safely back to the praetorium.

It was a short distance from the temple to his quarters, and Pilate took the remainder of the night to reflect on what he had heard and what he had experienced. He looked forward to responding in writing about the heavy burden of emotions that he had carried around for the past week or so since Jesus was first delivered to him. It was finally over, he felt. He discovered the truth about Jesus of Nazareth which troubled him unceasingly since the night the ordeal began. He had finally confirmed what he'd suspected in his own mind since the first night that Jesus was brought to him. He was not a Jew, nor a believer in their God, but the events that happened to him and to the people, in this peculiar place, he was now inextricably a part of. All he had now were his thoughts, emotions, and memories of the fateful day of Jesus' trial and crucifixion, which he would eventually write about and record, and place in the hall of records in the Roman praetorium at Jerusalem.

While Pilate sat pensively at his desk, he was interrupted by a centurion who entered and handed him a letter that was addressed to him from Herod the Tetrarch. Pilate received the letter and carefully looked it over. He thought nothing of the correspondence letter and he slowly opened it and began to read it, which read,

**Herod; to Pontius Pilate the Governor of Jerusalem. Peace.**

I presently and suddenly find myself in great anxiety. I write these things to you, that when you have heard them you may be grieved for me. For I have received communication from Rome that as my daughter Herodias, who is dear to me, was playing upon a pool of water which had ice upon it, it broke under her feet, and all her body went down into the ice and as she sank below the surface her head was severed and remained upon the surface of the ice. Behold now, I am told, that her mother has been holding her head upon her knees in her lap ever since the accident, and my whole house has been in great sorrow since that day. And now for my house am I grieved beyond my soul. For when I heard that the man Jesus was delivered to you in the night, I wished to come to you that maybe I might speak with him alone, and hear his words, whether they are like those of the sons of men. And I am certain today that because of the many evil things which were done by me to John the Baptist, and because I mocked the Christ, behold I now receive the just reward of righteousness, for I have shed much blood of other's children upon the earth. Therefore the judgments of God are righteous; for every man receives according to his thoughts, but because you were found worthy to see the God-man, therefore it becomes you to pray for me.

My son Azbonius also is in the agony of the hour of his death. And I too am in great affliction, and great trial, because I have contracted the dropsy. I am instantly now in great distress, because I persecuted the introducer of baptism by water, which was John. Therefore, my friend, behold that the judgments of God are righteous. And my wife, again, through all her grief for our daughter, is become blind with anguish [in her left eye], because we desired to blind the eye of righteousness. Truly, there is no peace to the doers of evil.

Now, if there be place for me to request of you, O Pilate, seeing that I was one time in power, see to it that you bury me carefully along with my household when the time comes. For it is right that we should be buried by you, rather than by the priests whom we venerate. For after a little while, vengeance shall overtake all those who oppose God.

Fare thee well, O Pilate, you and your wife Procla. I send you the earrings of my daughter and my own ring, that they may be a memorial of my decease. For in a short time, worms will begin to issue from my body, and lo, I will receive temporal judgment, and I am sorely afraid of the judgment to come. For in both, we stand before the works of the living God; but this judgment, which is temporal, is for a time, while that judgment which is to come, is forever.

**End of the letter to Pilate the Governor.**

Pilate was shaken by the news he received in the form of this letter from his old friend and colleague. He personally witnessed the terror of the eclipse, and the rising of the dead at Jesus' crucifixion, which was evidence enough that Jesus was innocently crucified upon the cross. Now, he was receiving information that further confirmed to him the righteous judgment of God, and the purity of the man Jesus. Pilate knew that he could've done more to prevent Jesus from being hanged on a cross, but what could he do now to help Herod? Again guilt, and his sense of responsibility consumed him, and he grieved for his friend, because the judgments of God against those who once opposed Jesus were again being fulfilled, this time through Herod and the apparent suffering of his family.

Pilate determined that he had vindicated himself from the sins of the Jews when he washed his hands in front of them days ago, and proclaimed his innocence from the blood of Jesus. He knew instinctively that from this point on his life would never be the same. A statesman he was, soldier of the Roman Empire, prefect and Governor of the Eastern province of Jerusalem. But none of those things could surmount what he had experienced and gone through since Jesus' trial. He was a man; a man who could not run away from his emotions or from his inherent duty to stand for what was true and real in his life.

He sat alone in his office chambers. It was a quiet and solemn time for the man who had put down many rebellions in the land of the Jews with the heaviest of hands. As prefect of Judah, he was accustomed at putting down any hint of revolt or insurrection. He now found himself irrevocably intertwined in a tragic series of events. He could not deny his role in the totality of them. His moral intuition would not allow him to deny his role in this continuously unfolding tragedy. It was a time of great reflection for Pilate concerning the events that lead him to this particular moment of introspection. He had fought in many battles, but none were more gripping than the battle he was fighting as a result of his role in the death of Jesus Christ.

He reread the letter he received from Herod the Tetrarch. He knew that what was happening to him was in part the result of Herod's political misdealings. He was seeing clearly, that all those people who opposed themselves to Jesus at the time of his trial, were soon to pay the just price of their acts against him. Herod was the living proof of this thought. He beheaded Jesus' cousin, John the

Baptist, and Herod's judgment was stated in the letter Pilate held in his hands, whose family was now being sorely punished for their acts of murder and contempt against Jesus, as well as John the Baptist. Though Pilate couldn't deny his anger toward Herod, he also felt a sense of growing pity toward him as well.

Pilate sat at his desk ready to respond in writing to Herod, feeling the weight of his friend's request to bury his family, which Herod cast on to him through the suffering and fear for the lives of his wife and young son. Pilate addressed his response to Herod, saying,

**Pilate to Herod the Tetrarch: Peace.**

Know and understand, that in the night when you had Jesus delivered up to me, I took pity on myself and testified by washing my hands that I was innocent concerning Jesus. For I perceived that you desired me to be associated with you in his crucifixion. But I have now also learned from the executioners, and from the soldiers who kept watch over his sepulcher, that he indeed did rise again from the dead. And I have especially confirmed for myself what was told me by my soldiers, that he appeared bodily in Galilee, in the same physical form, with the same voice, and the same doctrine, and with the same disciples, not having changed in anything but preaching with boldness his resurrection, and an everlasting kingdom.

Now Herod, behold, heaven and earth do rejoice. Surely you have seen, as I have, the great eclipse which occurred several days ago on the first day of the week? And you felt the earthquake, and the great light and thunder that was come from the heaven. And even Procla, my wife, is believing in the visions which appeared to her, when you sent Jesus to me that I should deliver him to the people of Israel, because of the ill intent they had toward him. When she heard that Jesus was risen, she went to Galilee to see for herself if what she heard was true. And she took with her Longinus and several other soldiers. Now while they were on the road into Galilee, they saw Jesus speaking with his disciples. And Jesus spoke to her, and asked her if she now indeed did believe on him? And he confirmed to her that all those who had perished and believed on him, would live again by means of his death. Jesus has broken the cords of death, and the gates of Sheol.

When Jesus thus spoke these words to Procla, she came and told me, weeping and in great anguish. Even the soldiers who accompanied her wept along with her, even though many of them were against Jesus and mocked him openly at the trial. They were also among those who beat him, and spat on him as he carried his cross up the hill to Golgotha. When I heard all these things of him being seen in the body I, again, took pity on myself, and put on a robe of mourning for I intended within myself to mourn for him whom I helped to put to death unjustly.

But I was compelled to do otherwise, so I gathered to myself fifty soldiers and we set out to Galilee to see Jesus for ourselves. And as we were traveling along on the road to Galilee, I testified these things against you, Herod, to my wife and to my company: that you are responsible for bringing these things upon me, and in that, you took counsel against me and constrained me to arm my hands against Jesus, and to judge him that judges all, and to scourge a just man, who is Lord of the just.

While we approached Galilee going along the road, the earth began to quake, and my entire company heard a great voice of thunder in heaven. When this happened I began to pray in my heart because I saw Jesus whom you delivered to me. And as we came near to him, I stepped down from my caravan and I fell on my face in subjection to him. I besought him that he would forgive me who set at judgment him who avenges all in truth. Procla, my wife came and did to him the same as I. Whereupon he proclaimed great words to us and proclaimed an everlasting kingdom from henceforth.

Nevertheless Herod, I am at odds with you; it was you, along with the children of Israel, who constrained me to do evil unto Jesus, and for this I asked for his pardon. Nevertheless, I receive your request to bury your family along with you, when that time comes. I will see to it myself that your son and wife receive the proper burials as you have requested of me. The earrings you have sent me I will keep as a memorial of your living. I wish all speed and diligence to your recovery. Be well, my friend.

**End of the Letter of Pilate to Herod;**

# CHAPTER 21

## Pilate's fate

Several weeks had come and gone, and uncharacteristically Pilate had not reported any of the details that he'd heard form Nicodemus and Joseph to Tiberius Caesar in his daily reports. It had been some time since the trial and crucifixion, and he was still quite overwhelmed by the enormity and the burden of his experiences, and the request to bury Herod's family. He was coming to grips with the idea that he could not expel himself from all the astonishing events that had taken place in his life recently and in the province in which he kept order as Governor.

Most of the Hebrew people were now settling back down into their normal routines. Perhaps these strange people were accustomed to the miracles that seemed to happen so readily to them in their land by the hand of their God. By now, it was well documented the miracles that

Jesus had performed in the land of Jews, but also the many miracles that God himself had performed in the presence of the people. Many of them were resigned to the fact that those miracles that happened at Jesus' crucifixion came from no other than from the hands of the God whom they worshipped.

Pilate knew now that the time had certainly come for him to address Caesar directly and to inform him completely about what happened concerning Jesus and his failure to litigate the trial with equity and objectivity. At the time of the trial Pilate was concerned more for himself, than he was for the welfare of Jesus (or for executing sound judgment during the trial), and he did not want to risk having to put down another upheaval by the Jews so close to the time of the Passover. He hoped that the High Holy Day would come and go with little disturbance. However, despite his desire and intention to maintain order, it was not to be. In fact, his decision to crucify Jesus unleashed a series of events that no one could have foreseen.

Pilate decided that it was now time for him to face his responsibilities to the empire, not knowing what fate awaited him as a consequence of his actions the day Jesus was tried and crucified. But his responsibility to the empire could no longer wait, and he addressed his correspondence to Tiberius Caesar, saying;

## Pontius Pilate to Tiberius Caesar the Emperor – Greeting,

Lord, Concerning Jesus whom I fully made known to you in my last letters, a bitter punishment has at length been inflicted by the will of the people, although I was unwilling and apprehensive to execute - the order of the Jews who demanded that Jesus be put to death. In good truth, no age had, nor will have, a man so good and strict. But the people made a wonderful effort against him; all their scribes, chief priests, and elders agreed to crucify him who was an ambassador of truth.

Many of the common people of the Jews, and many other of their prophets, like the Sibyls with us, attempted to persuade them to the contrary. But the people decided that he should be hanged upon the cross. And when he was dying, many supernatural signs appeared, and in the judgment of the people menaced the whole land with ruin. [His disciples flourish, not belying their master by their behavior and continence of life. Rather, in his name they are most beneficent.] However, had I not feared that a

184

sedition might arise among the multitude of the Jews who were confederate against him, perhaps this man might yet still be alive with us.

Although I was compelled by fidelity to the dignity of thy holiness, rather than led by my own inclination, I did not strive with all my might to prevent the sale and suffering of his righteous blood. I was convinced in my own mind that he was guiltless of every accusation brought against him unjustly. But through the maliciousness of men, and even as the scriptures of the Hebrews interpret to their own destruction, I sentenced him to be whipped and crucified.

Now when he was crucified, there was darkness over all the land, and the sun was obscured for half of the day, and the stars appeared but there was no luster seen in them. And the moon also lost its brightness, and the world of the departed was swallowed up so that the very sanctuary of the temple (as they call it) did not appear to the Jews themselves at their downfall. But, rather, they perceived a chasm in the earth where the sanctuary stood, and the rolling of successive thunder was heard therein.

Amid all this terror the dead appeared rising again, as the Jews themselves bore witness, and said it was Abraham, Isaac, and Jacob, and the twelve patriarchs, and Moses and Job, who had died before as they say some three thousand five hundred years ago. There were many whom I myself saw appearing in the body, and they made lamentation over the Jews because of their transgression which was committed by them, and because of the destruction of the Jews and their law.

When it was evening on the first day of the week, there came a sound from heaven, and the heaven became seven times more luminous than on all other days. And at the third hour of the night the sun appeared again more luminous than it had ever shone, lighting up the whole hemisphere. Lightning flashes suddenly came forth in a storm, and there were seen men lofty in stature crying out, and their voices were heard as that of exceedingly loud thunder saying, "Jesus that was crucified is risen again. Come up from Hades ye that were enslaved in the subterraneous recesses of Hades." The chasm in the earth was as if it had no bottom, but it was so that the very foundations of the earth appeared with those that shouted in heaven, and many Jews walked in the body among the dead that were raised. And Jesus, that raised up the dead and bound Hades, said, "Say unto my disciples, He goeth before you into Galilee, there shall you see him."

Many of the priests of the Jews died in the chasm of the earth, being swallowed up by the darkness thereof so that on the next day many of those who opposed Jesus were not to be found. Others saw the apparition of men rising again whom none of us had ever seen before. Therefore, being greatly astounded by that terror that overtook the people of Jerusalem, and being possessed with the most dreadful trembling, I have written what I saw at that time and sent to thy excellency. I have also inserted what was done against Jesus by the Jews, and sent it to thy divinity my lord. Farewell. The 5th of the calends of April.

**End of the letter of Pontius Pilate to the Emperor, Tiberius Caesar;**

When Pilate's correspondence to Caesar came to the city of the Romans, they were read to him aloud with no few of his servants and counselors standing in attendance. Upon hearing Pilate's letters, all who stood there were alarmed because through the transgression of Pilate, the darkness of the eclipse and the earthquake were both seen and felt in Rome and throughout the entire world.

Tiberius was filled with terror and anger against Pilate, and he commanded soldiers be sent to Jerusalem that Pilate should be arrested and brought to him as a prisoner. So the centurions did as was commanded them by the emperor, and they set sail across the water to Judaea to arrest Pilate for his crimes against Tiberius and the Roman state. When the soldiers arrived, they found Pilate in the praetorium, and the decree for his arrest from Tiberius was read to him by Lucianus, who was to now assume governorship over Jerusalem and all of Judaea in Pilate's stead.

Pilate, when confronted by the soldiers and centurions, was quickly and forcefully apprehended by them and taken into custody as prisoner of the Roman state for treason and for his crimes against the god-man Jesus. When he was brought back to the city of the Romans, word was reported to Tiberius that Pilate was come, had been imprisoned and was awaiting trial by Caesar's tribunal in the temple of the gods. Pilate spent his first days back in

Rome as a prisoner in a cold and damp cell reserved for common criminals.

The next day, Caesar summoned all the senators, his generals, and the entire multitude of his power to be witnesses at the trial of Pontius Pilate, and to inquire of him about his role and decision to put Jesus to death, whom he had clearly stated in his letters was unjustly whipped and put to death even though he was innocent of the crimes leveled against him by the Jews. Caesar sat in his judgment seat high above the senate, and the army, in the temple of the gods. He sat prepared to interrogate Pilate about his role in the death of Jesus of Nazareth.

Caesar ordered his soldiers to bring Pilate into the temple to face trial, the guards went and retrieved Pilate from his cell. Now, Pilate was prepared to stand in the same role under Caesar that Jesus stood in, a few months earlier under Pilate's power and jurisdiction. Caesar commanded that Pilate stand at the entrance of the temple, so that he not be allowed to stand in the temple of the gods, and defile it with his wickedness.

As Pilate stood at the entrance of the temple, Caesar began his trial and spoke boldly to Pilate and said to him, "O most impious Pilate, why when you saw such great signs done by that man whom you held prisoner, did you dare condemn him to be scourged and crucified? By daring to do such an evil deed against him, you have brought ruin upon my empire and the entire world."

Pilate said calmly and reverently to Caesar, "King and autocrat, I am not guilty of these things, neither am I guilty of the blood of Jesus of Nazareth. Rather it is the multitude of the Jews who are guilty of putting him to death. I, even I, at one point during his trial washed my hands in front of all those who stood and witnessed, signifying my innocence from his blood which they sought to shed."

Caesar said to Pilate, "Who are those Jews of whom you speak, and have mentioned in your writings?"

"Annas, Caiaphas, Gamaliel, Archelaus, Philip and all the multitude of Jews, both priests and elders," said Pilate.

Then Caesar said, "For what cause did you execute their purpose against him knowing that he was innocent of the charges they brought against him?"

Pilate said, "Lord, their nation is seditious, and insubordinate, and they are not submissive to thy power, O king, nor have they submitted to the power of their God."

Caesar said, "When they delivered him unto you, you ought to have secured him and sent him to me, and should not have consented with them to crucify such a man as this, who was just and wrought such great and good miracles, as you have stated. For by the multitude of such miracles, this man Jesus was manifested to be the Christ, and also the King of the Jews, is this not true?"

Pilate then said, "Indeed, I believed him to be the king of the Jews, as he indeed stated. But Caiaphas and Annas, being chief among them, denied that claim fervently, and were predisposed against him."

Then, just at the moment when Caesar asked Pilate, and spoke the name Jesus Christ in the temple of the Roman gods, the ground within the temple began to quake, and all the multitude of the gods and statues that were exalted and stood in the temple began to wobble, and all the statues and idols of the Roman gods, which were erected high above the seat of the emperor, began to fall down one after another in the temple where Caesar sat with his senate, in the extravagance of his power, and shattered like dust right before his eyes. This quake that befell the Roman gods lasted for several minutes, long enough to leave no question in the minds of the senators and soldiers as to what was happening.

While Pilate stood in the midst of the entrance of the temple of the gods and felt the quake and witnessed the fall of the Roman gods, he thought back vividly to the trial, and to what Jesus had said to him, when he said, "All power belongs to God." Pilate began to feel the same fear that overcame him at the time of Jesus' trial. He knew too well the power that came from the name Jesus Christ, even the powers that were given to him at the time of his crucifixion, and the power of his word. Pilate heard first-hand the testimony of the many miracles Jesus did among the people. He witnessed those miracles that appeared in the sky over Jerusalem when Jesus lay dying on the cross. All the people and senators who sat in attendance in the temple also became filled with fear from the power of the quake, and trembled at the utterance of the name Jesus Christ and at the fall of all the gods when his name was mentioned in their temple.

And they, being seized with trepidation, murmured among themselves and began to flee from the temple, and went away every man to his house wondering in amazement at what they witnessed. Only Caesar and his most loyal guards and soldiers remained in the temple once the quaking ceased. Those others who remained in the temple marveled at the devastation inside. Caesar, seeing the destruction, and the fear that overcame those who attended, commanded that Pilate be bound hand and foot, and be secured safely in his cell, so that he might return and face trial in the morning about the truth of the man Jesus.

The next morning Caesar again sat in his power in the capitol building inside Rome, and he assembled again the senate and his generals to be witness to Pilate's trial. When the soldiers brought Pilate into the capitol building from his cell, they sat him down in front of Caesar and all the senators and generals, shackled hand and foot.

Caesar started in on Pilate and said to him, "Tell now the truth, most impious Pilate, for through your irreverent deeds that you did commit against Jesus, the doing of your evil works are manifested here in the city of my dominion in that even the gods which we honor are all brought to ruin. So tell me now, who is this Jesus that you crucified, for his name alone has destroyed the gods of our people?"

Pilate said to Tiberius, "Verily it is Jesus of Nazareth, from a certain city of the Jews. And his record is true; for even I myself was convinced by his works that he was greater than all the gods whom we worship."

Caesar said to Pilate, "Seeing that he was so great, for what cause then did you perpetrate against him such daring and doing, not being ignorant of him, thus assuredly designing such mischief to my government?"

"I did it because of the transgression and sedition of the lawless and ungodly Jews," answered Pilate.

"Because of the lawless and ungodly Jews?" questioned Caesar. He sat and thought for a moment, thinking upon what Pilate said to him. Then being filled with curiosity, he leaned over and quietly held council with a couple of the senators and officers who sat near to him, and he reckoned with them that a decree should be written against the seditious Jews who were complicit with Pilate in putting Jesus to death. Then Caesar reconvened and spoke to all those assembled in the capitol building, and he ordered one of his scribes to record the words of his decree. He said,

**To Lucianus, who now holdeth the first place in the East Country. Greeting.**

I have been informed of the audacity perpetrated recently by the Jews inhabiting Jerusalem and the cities round about, and their lawless doing, how they compelled Pilate (then governor of the East Country) to crucify a certain god called Jesus, through which great transgression of theirs the world was darkened and drawn into ruin. Therefore, I determine, that a body of soldiers go to them at once and proclaim to them their subjection to bondage by this decree. By obeying and proceeding against them, and scattering them abroad in all nations, enslave them and drive their nation from all of Judaea; and as soon as possible show, wherever this decree has not yet appeared, that they are godless, full of evil, and the enemies of Tiberius Caesar and the Empire of Rome, from this day forth.

**End of the decree against the Jews given by Tiberius Caesar Supreme Emperor of Rome;**

When Tiberius finished speaking the words of his decree, he ordered a contingent of centurions to prepare

195

their soldiers to set sail across the water and deliver his words to Lucianus in the East Country. When the soldiers arrived in Jerusalem they delivered the decree to Lucianus. Then Lucianus, through fear of the decree of Caesar, obeyed the words of the decree, and he began to lay waste to all the nation of the Jews in Jerusalem and to the cities round about Jerusalem. Through the power of the decree, he caused those Jews that remained alive in Judaea to be taken into slavery along with those that were scattered among the nations of the Gentiles, that it might be known by Caesar that all these things had been executed by Lucianus against the Jews in the East Country as to please the emperor through his deeds.

Once Caesar made the decree, he was resolved in his mind to have Pilate put to death. He commanded a certain captain of the Roman Legion named Albius, that on the next day he was to execute Pilate by death of beheading. In front of the senate and all the generals of his army, Tiberius told Albius, "Tomorrow, the traitor of the Roman Empire, Pontius Pilate, former Governor of the Eastern Province of Jerusalem, will sacrifice his life and have his head cut off upon your decree. As he once laid hands upon the just-man that is called Christ, he shall also fall in like manner, and find no deliverance for his soul."

Pilate was deeply moved, but he stood speechless in front of Caesar and the senate, and the generals. He was not sure what he could say at this point, he stayed silent. Tiberius was resigned to the fact that Pilate was guilty of putting Jesus to death unjustly. Pilate could not deny, indeed, that he hadn't done exactly that, despite the fact that he found no guilt in him, and that he publicly absolved himself of Jesus' innocence. He still made the decision to have Jesus whipped and crucified. And it was through his own words, he admitted, that he did not strive against Caiaphas and the rest of the Jews as strongly as he should have. He thought in his mind that the punishment he was now condemned to was just in the sense that he was to pay with his life for taking the life of Jesus, who was innocent.

Procla, witnessing her husband's arrested at the hands of the roman soldiers, and taken prisoner by Caesar's decree, gathered together her servants and hand-maidens and set sail across the water to Rome to be a part of the final fate of her husband. She stood witness on both days of his trial. She heard Caesar's words condemning Pilate to death. And Pilate was again forcefully seized and returned back to his cell shackled by his hands and feet, where he was held until the morning when he would confront the final moments of his life.

That night, while Pilate sat quietly in his cold dimly lit cell, he continued to replay the events of the crucifixion. Only now could he justify the events that had led him to this point. The events of his life had completely come full circle: from leading a trial against Jesus, which was a witch hunt to kill the king of Jews, to witnessing with his own eyes Jesus resurrected in the same form which he was at the trial, to confronting Annas and Caiaphas and the other priests to learn the truth about Jesus as was told by the prophets of the Jews in the book of the Lord. Now he sat alone in his cell convicted of treason. He exonerated himself from all guilt and accountability for Jesus' death. He showed his innocence from the blood of Jesus by washing his hands and declaring openly that he did not agree with the enraged Jews who were determined to see Jesus crucified.

But now he was seeing his own life through the eyes of Jesus Christ. Despite his allegiance to the empire, and to the Roman legion as a soldier and equestrian, he was convicted of treason against the empire like a common criminal. He knew he could've done more to prevent the shedding of innocent blood, but there was nothing he could do to reverse his decision. He made peace with Jesus, both he and Procla, but now his crimes and punishment were against the empire and against Tiberius, not Jesus.

While he sat quietly in his cell with his mind and thoughts, he turned and knelt on the cold damp floor of the cell and prostrated himself to the God of heaven, and he began to pray to the God whom he had held prisoner. He prayed to the Lord Jesus. As he prayed, he prayed fervently to the Lord, saying, "O Lord Jesus, destroy not my soul along with those of the wicked Hebrews, for I would not have laid hands upon you, but by the nation of lawless Jews I was compelled to act in like manner, because they provoked sedition against me. But you know, Lord, that what I did was done in ignorance. Destroy me not, therefore, O Lord, for this my sin. Neither, Lord, be mindful of the evil that is in me, and in your servant Procla, who has travelled from the east country, eschewing all danger for her own life, and stands with me in the hour of my death. Even to her be merciful, O Lord, whom you have taught to prophecy that you might be nailed to the cross. Do not punish her as a result of my sin, but forgive us both, and number us in the portion of your faithful ones."

Now behold, while Pilate sat kneeling in prayer, brought to tears by the weight of his mind, there came a voice from heaven that only Pilate perceived. The voice was as if it were there inside the cell. And when the voice spoke to him, it lighted the dim wet cell where he was imprisoned, and the voice spoke clearly unto him, saying, "O Pilate, all the generations and all the families of the Gentiles shall call you blessed, because under your dominion were fulfilled all the things that were spoken by the prophets concerning me. And you must also appear as witness, at my second coming when I shall judge the twelve tribes of Israel, and those who have not confessed my name."

Pilate lifted his head up to see the image of the voice that appeared before him. But as suddenly as the light appeared before him, lighting the darkness of the cell, it was gone, and the darkness of the damp cell returned to Pilate's eyes. The image of the voice appeared and disappeared in the fleeting of a moment. Pilate wept out of frustration because of the voice that had come and gone in a moment of time. He wept because he was coming to terms with his fate. He was no longer a statesman, nor a soldier. He was no longer Governor, but rather a common man, who, like the common people, had believed the testimony of Jesus Christ.

Jesus was condemned by his people, whom he had come to save from their sins. Pilate was now condemned to death, at the hands and behest of Caesar and the Roman people. He sympathized with Jesus' fate while he was held prisoner the night before his death. He saw Jesus' life now reflected in his own life. In some strange way, he felt relief that his fate was the same as that of Jesus Christ, whom he knew to be innocent of the crimes brought against him, as well. Even though his life was to end early the next morning, his faith was confirmed that night. Pilate lay on the floor of his cell, until he fell asleep and was found by the centurion in the morning, sleeping where he once prayed.

As Pilate was taken from his cell, and led to the execution area, he said nothing to the soldiers who came to retrieve him. His expression remained the same from the time he walked out of his cell, to the time his head was placed inside the guillotine. There was no going back. He was living the last moments of his life. He never predicted that his life would end this way. He had never, before now, believed in the afterlife. But he witnessed Jesus alive after his death, and he was told that he was to stand with Jesus at his second coming.

When he walked into the execution area, he looked and saw Procla who stood there prepared to receive his fate. She was faithful to all they had experienced. She was faithful to the vision she had concerning Jesus and her husband. The events of the trial and crucifixion were as profound to her as they were to him.

Pilate was led in front of Tiberius Caesar. Caesar stood up in the Glory of his empire and spoke to Pilate, saying, "You have been found guilty of treason against the state of Rome for your negligent acts against the god-man Jesus. And for that, you will face death by beheading this day." Pilate stood there dutifully and said nothing, and he was quickly led away to the guillotine by the soldiers who led him in from his cell. For the first time he feared for life. He thought about Procla and remembered the words she spoke to him, which were now prophetic and true.

He approached the guillotine silently and was placed to his knees by the soldiers. Albius the centurion stood to the side waiting to execute the order to take Pilate's life. Once he was secured into the guillotine, the soldiers backed away from him, and Albius looked up toward Tiberius to receive the final order to execute his duty to the empire. Upon receiving Caesar's final order,

Albius grabbed hold of the rope and pulled the cord of the heavy blade, which fell upon Pilate's neck, severing his head from his body. His head rolled and laid there on the ground.

Once Pilate's head was severed there was a small silence, then a soft murmur of voices came from all those in the audience. As the large crowd of on-lookers began to quietly murmur about witnessing Pilate's beheading, an angel of the Lord, slowly and silently, descended from the sky ready to receive Pilate's head. No one in the audience perceived the angel descending from the sky (not Caesar, or his generals). But Procla perceived the coming of the angel of the Lord, and once she realized that she had perceived the Lord's angel descending from the sky, she became filled with the spirit of the Lord, and forthwith gave up the ghost and fell down dead just like her husband.

Pilate's headless body was removed from the guillotine and given over to his family who had come from the lands north of Rome to be witness to his execution. Procla's body was carried away by her hand-maidens and placed in the chariot in which she rode. Pilate's body was taken by his family and later buried in the field of Pontii, where his forefathers were buried. And there he was laid and intended to rest until Jesus returned the second time to fulfill his word to him at the coming of his kingdom.